Penny in Space

FABER-CASTELL
since 1761

Penny the Pencil has a proud heritage. She is made by the leading pencil manufacturer in the world, Faber-Castell. The Faber-Castell family have been making pencils for eight generations. It all started in a small workshop in Germany in 1761 and now the company employs 5,500 people worldwide. The company is run by Count Anton Wolfgang von Faber-Castell.

Faber-Castell is a company with great flair and vision. It is in the *Guinness Book of Records* for creating the world's tallest pencil at almost twenty metres high and has also made the most expensive pencil ever. The Grip 2001 pencil brings together these elements of design, quality and innovation. It has won many international awards. With its unique soft grip zone and comfortable triangular shape it has become a worldwide classic.

Penny in Space

EILEEN O'HELY
Illustrated by Nicky Phelan

MERCIER PRESS
IRISH PUBLISHER – IRISH STORY

Main Characters

The Space Camp Tutors

Contents

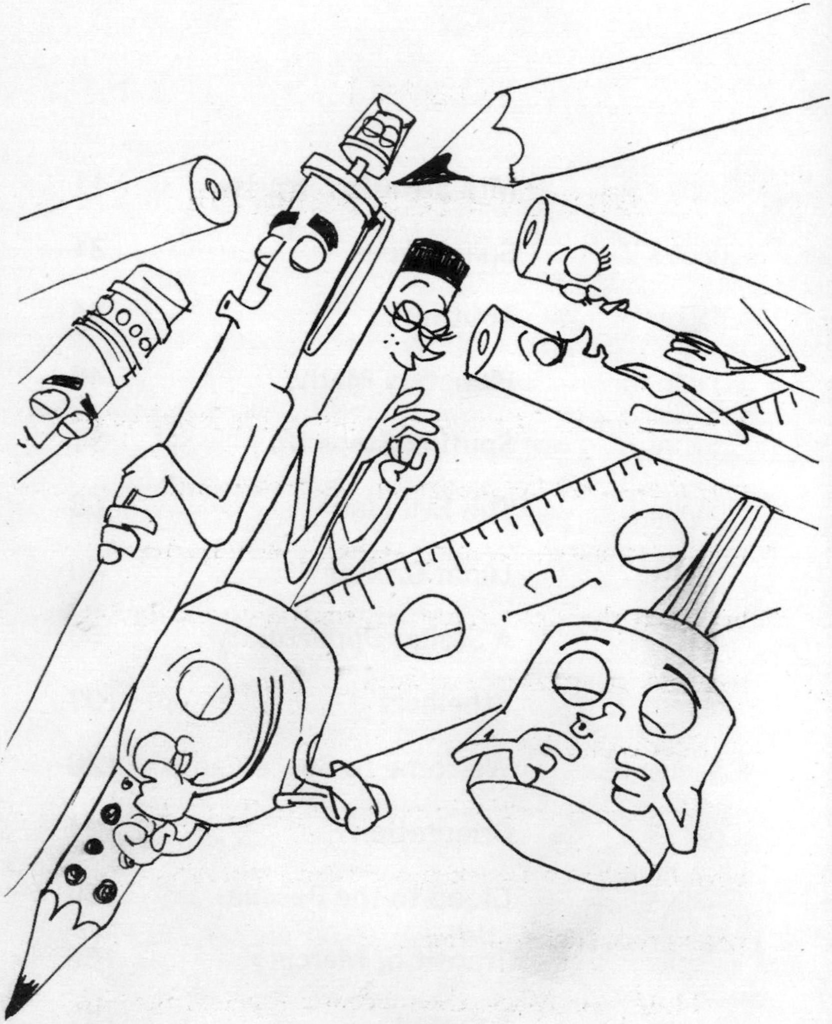

Chapter 1

Mrs Sword's Surprise

It was a typical Monday morning inside Ralph's pencil case. All the pencils and other writing implements were sleeping soundly, having gone to bed early the night before in preparation for the big week ahead of them at school.

Suddenly, a bell rang.

'What was that?' said Penny, a grey lead pencil with bubbles on her skirt, to the red mechanical pencil that lay beside her.

'Huh?' said Mack, the mechanical pencil sleepily.

'THE BELL'S RUNG AND WE'RE ALL STILL ASLEEP!' yelled Penny, leaping up out of bed.

'We won't all be asleep for long if you keep that racket up,' said Gloop, the wise old bottle of correction fluid lying on Penny's other side. 'What's the matter, Penny?'

'The bell rang. Didn't you hear it?' said Penny, shaking the pencils around her awake. 'Ralph's going to open the zip any second. We have to be ready!'

'What time is it, Jade?' yawned a tall, orange pencil to the short, green pencil beside it.

'Only eight o'clock, Amber,' replied Jade snoozily.

'But school doesn't start until nine. What's Penny doing waking us all up?' asked Amber.

'Daylight savings?' suggested Jade.

'In the middle of January?' said Amber.

'Penny, stop it,' said Gloop before Penny could disturb any more of the slumbering pencils. 'I think you'll find that wasn't the school bell. We haven't even left Ralph's bedroom yet.'

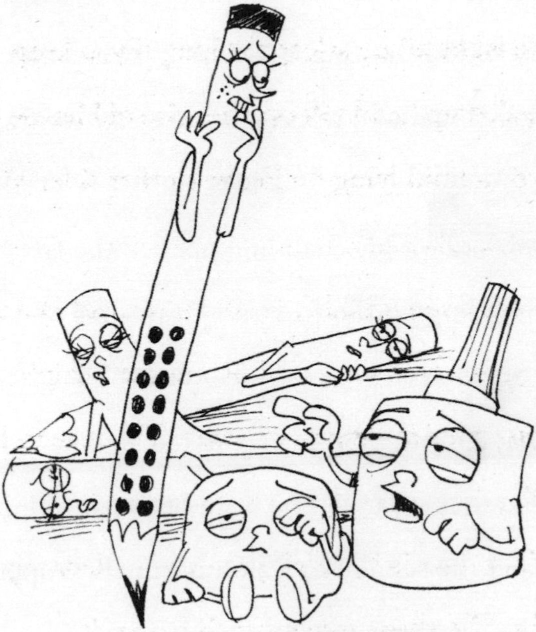

'Then what was it?' asked Smudge, Ralph's little rubber who had also been woken up by all the commotion.

'My guess is the doorbell,' said Gloop.

*

Downstairs, Ralph was spooning cereal into his mouth when the doorbell rang a second time.

'Ralph, would you be a love and see who's at the

door?' asked his mother, who was in the middle of ironing a blouse and in no fit state to answer the door.

Ralph slid off his chair and opened the front door. Standing on the front porch was his best friend Sarah.

'What are you doing here?' asked Ralph, surprised to see Sarah. She lived between Ralph's house and the school, so Ralph normally dropped by her house on his way to school.

'I just wanted to make sure you weren't running late for school,' said Sarah, her face flushed and her eyes shining.

'But it's only eight o'clock …' said Ralph, scratching his unbrushed hair.

'I know,' said Sarah, walking inside and sitting at the breakfast table. 'But on Friday afternoon Mrs Sword said she had a surprise for us, remember?'

Ralph thought hard. He'd climbed a lot of trees and played loads of computer games since Friday.

'Sort of ...' he said uncertainly.

'Well, hurry up then!' said Sarah. 'We don't want to be late, just in case it's another chocolate cake.'

Liking the sound of chocolate cake much more than fibre-enriched, cardboard-tasting cereal, Ralph tipped the rest of his breakfast – which had now gone soggy – down the sink so his mother wouldn't notice, and ran upstairs to brush his teeth and grab his schoolbag.

'Bye, Mum!' yelled Ralph as he and Sarah left for school.

'What do you think the surprise might be?' Sarah asked him as they hurried along the footpath.

'I haven't really thought about it,' admitted Ralph.

'Well I have,' said Sarah. 'I went to the library and looked up a reference book and lots of exciting things happened this week in history. The first dinosaur was discovered, so we might go on an excursion to the Natural History Museum ...'

'Or get to watch *Jurassic Park*!' said Ralph excitedly.

'Or,' continued Sarah, annoyed at the interruption, 'Isaac Newton was born ...'

'Who's he?' asked Ralph.

'Only the guy who discovered gravity,' tutted Sarah, 'so we might get to do a project on famous scientists ...'

'Or we could go to a theme park and do experiments with gravity on a rollercoaster!' said Ralph.

'I hardly think so,' said Sarah disapprovingly.

'We'd need our parents to sign permission slips if we were going on an excursion to a theme park.'

'Well,' said Ralph, 'we'd still need permission slips to go to the museum, so your guess is wrong too!'

'Hmm …' said Sarah thoughtfully. 'Whatever it is, it must be happening at school.'

'Oh, no,' said Ralph, slapping a hand to his forehead. 'Mrs Payne's coming back.'

'I don't think so,' said Sarah, shuddering at the thought of their old Health teacher. 'Mrs Sword didn't say anything about bringing our sports clothes.'

'Phew!' said Ralph. 'Then what could it be?'

'I don't know, but we're almost there, so let's find out!'

While the other children played in the playground, Sarah and Ralph ran up the steps into the school building and along the corridor to their classroom.

'The door's locked,' said Sarah, pulling on the handle.

'And there's a curtain over the window so we can't see in,' said Ralph.

'Maybe we're going to have another surprise visitor, like Rick O'Shea, and he's in there right now!' squeaked Sarah with excitement.

'If the door's locked, how did he get in there?' said Ralph.

'Oh, I don't know,' said Sarah. 'He plays a cop on TV. He probably knows all sorts of ways to sneak into a locked room.'

Ralph rolled his eyes. Finally the bell rang and the *click-clack* of Mrs Sword's heels could be heard coming down the corridor from the staff room. Mrs Sword unlocked the classroom door, but stood holding it shut until all the children had come in from the playground.

'Good morning, class. I hope you had a good weekend,' she said opening the door. 'Welcome to Space Week!'

Chapter 2

Space Week

The children standing closest to the door, including Ralph and Sarah, couldn't believe their eyes. The entire classroom was covered in black material with stars on it. There was a big sun drawn in yellow chalk on the blackboard, and mobiles of the planets were hanging from the roof. Stepping into the classroom really felt like stepping into space.

'This is better than anything I imagined,' said Sarah, taking her seat and looking around the classroom with amazement.

'I'm bringing my remote control Lunar Rover in tomorrow!' said Ralph.

'And I'll help you blast it into space,' muttered Bert, the bully who sat behind Ralph and Sarah.

'What was that?' said Ralph, turning around and narrowing his eyes at Bert's evil smirk.

'You'll find out,' said Bert nastily.

'Ralph!' said Mrs Sword. 'Turn around and face

the front or you'll find yourself spending Space Week outside the headmaster's office.'

Bert sniggered as Ralph sat forward once again, giving his chair a kick for good measure.

'Now,' said Mrs Sword. 'This week we'll be learning all about …'

'Space!' said Lucy Williams eagerly.

'Thank you, Lucy,' said Mrs Sword. 'We'll be learning about space and space travel.'

'Oh, boy!' said Ralph, knowing that his remote

control Lunar Rover would definitely get him extra marks at Show and Tell the next day.

'Your project, due on Friday, is to come up with your own design for a rocket,' continued Mrs Sword. 'And on Friday morning we'll be having a visit from somebody who's actually been in space!'

The whole class burst into excited chatter.

'But first, my budding astronauts,' said Mrs Sword once everyone had calmed down, 'we're going to learn a little bit about the solar system. Can anybody tell me what the solar system is?'

Everyone in the class turned to Sarah, who, as usual, had her hand up.

'Nobody else knows? Not even a guess?' asked

Mrs Sword, looking around at the other children. 'Very well then, Sarah.'

'The solar system is the system of the sun and eight planets that orbit around it, named after Sol, the Roman sun god,' said Sarah.

'Thank you, Sarah,' said Mrs Sword. 'Now, can somebody else tell me the names of any of the eight planets?'

This time, lots of children put their hands up.

'Ciara,' said Mrs Sword, pointing to the girl who sat in front of Ralph and Sarah.

'Saturn. It's the pretty one with the rings,' Ciara said, pointing to the planet hanging above her head.

'That's right, Ciara,' said Mrs Sword, looking around the room for another child with their hand up. 'Malcolm.'

'Jupiter,' said Malcolm. 'It's got a big, red spot.'

'Very good,' said Mrs Sword. 'And the red spot is

a lot bigger than the Earth,' she added. 'Seán?'

'The sun,' said Seán.

'I'm afraid the sun isn't actually a planet, Seán,' said Mrs Sword.

'What is it then?' asked Seán.

'It's a star,' said Mrs Sword.

'But it can't be,' argued Seán. 'It's big and yellow and you can see it in the daytime.'

'That's true,' said Mrs Sword. 'But the sun is actually quite a small star. It only looks big because we're so close to it.'

'How close?' asked Ralph.

'Okay, everybody put your imagining caps on,' said Mrs Sword.

The children closed their eyes and mimed putting on hats.

'The sun is around one hundred and fifty million kilometres away,' said Mrs Sword.

Ralph's eyes flew open.

'That's not close!' he said. 'Even if you travelled at 100 kilometres an hour, it would take you … um … a really long time to get there!'

'That's true,' said Mrs Sword. 'But if you travelled at the speed of light, like sunlight does, it'd only take you eight minutes.'

'Wow!' said the class.

'What about the other stars?' asked Sarah. 'How long does it take to get to them?'

'Well,' said Mrs Sword, 'the next closest star is so far away, that even if you travelled at the speed of light, it'd take you four years to get there.'

'Ooh,' said the class, utterly amazed by how big space was.

'What's in between us and the stars?' asked Lucy.

'Nothing,' said Mrs Sword. 'That's why it's called space.'

Mrs Sword gave the children a few moments to get used to the idea of the empty nothingness of space.

'So,' she said, clapping her hands. 'Back to the solar system. Who can tell me the name of another planet?'

'Mars,' said Bert. 'It's got Martians on it.'

'Er, as far as we know, there aren't any Martians,' said Mrs Sword.

'But there are lots of movies about them,' said Bert. 'They've got green blood …'

'You can't believe everything you see in the movies,' said Mrs Sword. 'After all, there are plenty of movies about talking animals, but they don't exist, do they?'

'My uncle has a talking parrot,' said Ciara. 'It says all sorts of swear words like ...'

'If we could get back to the solar system,' interrupted Mrs Sword loudly. 'What other planets are there?'

'Earth,' said Sarah.

'Very good,' said Mrs Sword. 'What else?'

'Pluto,' said Ralph.

'I'm afraid not,' said Mrs Sword. 'Pluto used to be called a planet, but now astronomers think it's too small, so they're calling it a dwarf planet instead. Any others?'

The class sat quietly. No one else could think of another planet.

'We're still missing four of them,' prompted Mrs Sword. Nobody even put up their hand to guess.

'All right then,' said Mrs Sword, picking up a big pile of plastic-covered books from her desk and handing them out. 'These are your Space Week packs. Each of them has a booklet full of important space facts – including the other four planets in the solar system – and a special astronaut pen.'

'What's an astronaut pen?' Ralph asked Sarah as Mrs Sword handed them their Space Week packs.

'It says it's a special anti-gravity pen that can write upside-down and in the weightless environment of space,' said Sarah, reading the blurb on the cover.

'Oh, goody!' said Ralph. 'Do you think that we'll get to test it in our rockets?'

'We're just designing the rockets,' said Sarah. 'We're not actually going to fly into space with them.'

'We might get to,' said Ralph hotly.

'Not by the end of the week,' said Sarah.

'Maybe not,' said Ralph. 'But that doesn't mean I can't build my rocket on the weekend, or over the holidays, once my design is finished.'

Sarah rolled her eyes.

'Ralph, do you have any idea how long it takes to build a rocket, or how much fuel it takes to launch it into outer space?' said Sarah.

'No,' said Ralph, 'how much fuel would it take to launch it into outer space?'

'I don't know,' said Sarah in a small voice.

'You don't know?' said Ralph, quite loudly, as he was used to Sarah knowing the answer to everything.

'You don't know! You don't know!' taunted Bert from behind them.

'Bert, do you even know what we're talking about?' said Sarah.

'No,' said Bert. 'But that doesn't matter because you don't know it! You're so stupid.'

'I'd rather be stupid than ugly,' said Ralph, doing his best to defend Sarah in front of the bully.

'Well, you've hit the jackpot,' said Bert nastily.

Chapter 3

Sputink

Inside the pencil case, Penny and the rest of Ralph's writing implements had been lined up by the zip in neat rows ever since the start of school bell went.

'What's taking him so long?' moaned Penny impatiently.

'Didn't Mrs Sword say something about a surprise last thing on Friday?' asked Smudge.

'Well it's a very slow surprise,' said Penny as the bell for morning break went.

'Shh!' warned Gloop as the pencil case wobbled and the zip began to open.

Penny shuffled to the front of all the other

pencils to make it easier for Ralph to grab her. But instead of Ralph's empty hand coming to fetch her, a brand new implement entered the pencil case, flying slowly above the heads of the others.

'Bleep … bleep … bleep …' bleeped the newcomer as it orbited around the pencil case. Then it lifted an arm to its mouth and started talking.

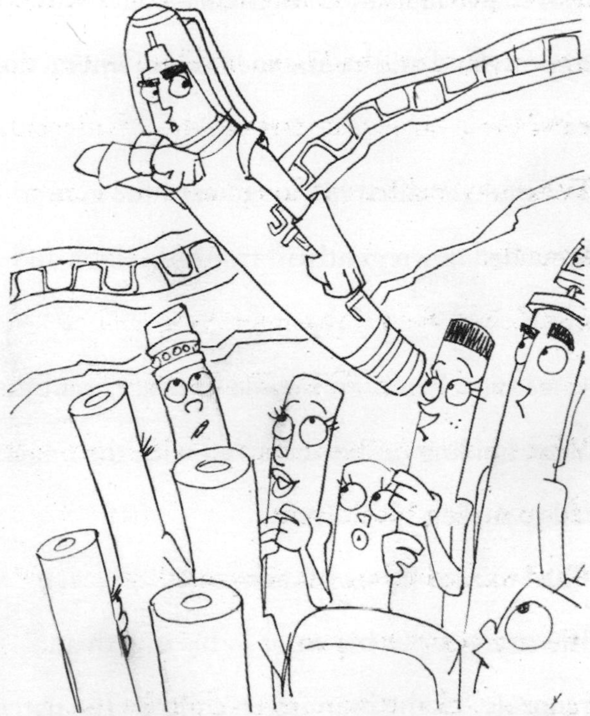

'Mission control, mission control, this is Sputink. Come in.'

In response, there was a hiss of static from the small device on its wrist.

'I appear to have reached an inhabited asteroid,' continued the newcomer. 'The natives look penciloid, but not hostile. I repeat, not hostile. I think I have identified their chieftain. I will attempt to land and commence verbal interaction. Over.'

The stranger tilted his toe toward the ground and touched down gently in front of Gloop and Penny.

'Greetings, Penlings. I come in peace,' said the stranger, holding up his left hand with the fingers paired to make a 'V'.

'Glad to hear it,' said Gloop.

The stranger put his wrist to his mouth and said quickly, 'Come in, mission control. The natives appear receptive and versed in the universal language of Penglish.'

'We call it English,' said Mack, leaning over towards the stranger's wrist.

'There appear to be both male and female of the species, and the male seems more aggressive …'

'Who are you calling aggressive?' demanded Mack.

'Calm down Mack,' said Penny, putting a hand on Mack's shoulder.

'… yet the female is more dominant,' continued the stranger.

'I'll show you who's dominant!' said Mack with his fists up.

‘Cool it, Mack,’ said Gloop.

‘They also appear to address each other by name, or else the second person singular of their language is “mack”.’

‘Speaking of names,’ said Gloop, growing tired of the stranger acting as though he was making a wildlife documentary, ‘do you have one?’

‘The chieftain has asked me a direct question. I must respond, or face retribution from the entire tribe. Report temporarily suspended as I engage in chit chat with the chieftain,’ said the stranger, finally pulling his wrist away from his face and attempting to smile.

‘I am Sputink,’ he said slowly and loudly.

‘Nice to meet you, Sputink,’ said Gloop, putting forward his hand to shake. ‘I’m Gloop, this is Penny, Mack, Smudge and the coloured pencils.’

Sputink looked at Gloop’s hand distrustfully before shaking it.

‘What are you doing here, Sputink?’ asked Penny.

‘My fleet has been dispatched to gather information on life-forms in this local cluster of asteroids,’ said Sputink.

‘Did you understand a word of that?’ Mack whispered to Smudge.

‘It makes sense if you swap “asteroid” for “pencil case” and “life-form” for “writing implement”,’ said Smudge, after taking a moment to think.

Mack thought for a moment, still didn’t get it, but nodded so as not to look stupid.

‘How many in your fleet?’ asked Gloop.

‘Thirty,’ said Sputink.

Mack finally understood what Smudge had said – there were thirty children in the class with thirty pencil cases.

‘What do you intend to do with the information you gather?’ continued Gloop.

'Add it to our *Encyclopedia Universa* under L for lesser life-forms,' said Sputink.

'Lesser life-forms?' said Penny, narrowing her eyes.

'Why yes! We space pens are the most advanced species in the cosmos,' said Sputink, matter-of-factly.

'Really?' said Penny.

'Really,' said Sputink. 'I can write upside-down …'

'So can I,' said Penny.

'Underwater …'

'Me too.'

'And my ink is immune to being erased by

beings such as this little fellow here,' said Sputink, scratching Smudge under the chin and making him giggle.

'Hmph,' said Penny. 'What if you make a mistake?'

'A mistake?' laughed Sputink. 'Advanced life-forms such as I do not make mistakes.'

'Just say the person writing with you does?' asked Penny.

Sputink frowned.

'What you are saying does not compute,' he said. 'Nobody writes with me. I choose when and what I write myself.'

'Not if you're in this pencil case you don't,' said Penny. 'You write exactly what Ralph wants to write, the way he wants to write it, and you don't correct his mistakes. Otherwise he'll never learn how to spell or do maths for himself.'

'Ralph? What's a Ralph?' asked Sputink.

'The little boy who owns us,' said Penny.

Sputink looked at her blankly.

'You know, red hair? Freckles?'

'You mean the humanoid?' asked Sputink.

'I guess so,' said Penny.

'I'm no slave to humanoids,' laughed Sputink. 'I'm on an important scientific mission …'

But Sputink was interrupted by the bell ringing to signal the end of playtime. All Ralph's writing implements stopped milling around Sputink and assembled into their neat rows.

Sputink watched them, then spoke into his communicator. 'Mission Control, Mission Control. This is Sputink resuming communications. I appear to have landed among a slave race who serve a humanoid called Ralph and exhibit zombie-like behaviour at the sound of a bell.'

'Shh!' hissed Penny.

'One could almost say they fear the bell.'

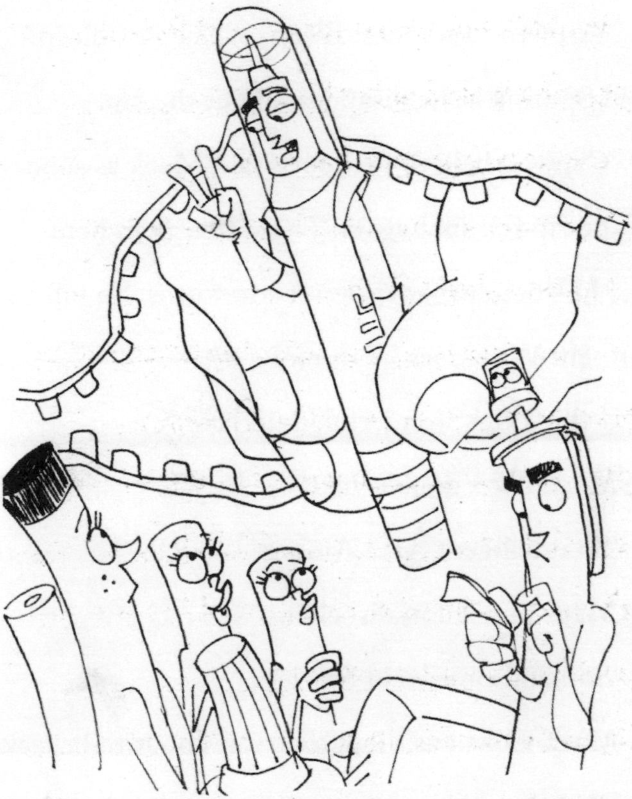

'Give me that,' said Mack, wrenching the communicator off Sputink's wrist.

At that moment the zip opened and Ralph's hand entered the pencil case. Instead of picking up Penny or Mack, Ralph's fingers closed around Sputink.

'Farewell, comrades! Bleep ... bleep ... bleep,' said Sputink as he disappeared out the zip.

'Can you believe that guy?' said Mack as soon as the zip fell shut again. 'Just waltzing in here like he's better than us lesser life-forms. So full of himself! Who does he think he is?'

'I think he's wonderful,' said Jade.

Mack did a double-take.

'So intelligent,' said Amber.

Mack blinked in disbelief.

'So handsome,' said Scarlet.

Mack looked as though he was about to be sick.

'Does Sputink remind you of someone else when he first arrived in the pencil case?' Gloop whispered to Penny, nodding in Mack's direction. Penny giggled.

'But Mack turned out to be okay in the end,' said Penny.

'Unlikely as it seems right now, Sputink may turn out to be okay too,' said Gloop.

'I don't know. I don't like his attitude, calling us all lesser life-forms. It reminds me of somebody else,' said Penny, shuddering.

'I know who you mean,' said Gloop. 'But Penny, I think it's time you stopped worrying about Black Texta. We got rid of him for good last time, remember?'

'You really think so?' asked Penny doubtfully.

'I'm sure of it,' said Gloop. 'Now let's keep an eye on what's going on out in the classroom. If Ralph's using that space pen, he'll be needing our help sooner rather than later.'

Chapter 4

Planetary Maths

As Penny peered out over the zip, the scene in front of her made all thoughts of Black Texta disappear instantly.

'Gloop?' said Penny. 'Are we really in outer space?'

Gloop laughed.

'No. It's Space Week. Mrs Sword has just decorated the classroom to make it look like we're in outer space,' said Gloop.

'She did a pretty good job,' said Penny, very impressed.

'You should have seen what it was like for

Underwater Week. There were fish, coral and even a giant squid!'

Penny looked at the space decorations with even more amazement than the children when they'd first walked into the classroom that morning. She was actually glad that Ralph had chosen the space pen to write with, as Penny was far too fascinated by the decorations to concentrate on schoolwork.

In Ralph's hand, Sputink was looking most annoyed.

'Bleep ... bleep ... humanoid what are you ... bleep ... doing?' yelled Sputink.

But Ralph, being human, couldn't hear anything Sputink – or any other pen or pencil – said.

'I think our friend now knows how it feels to be a lesser life-form,' observed Gloop. 'That should bring him down to earth.'

Ralph was also looking annoyed. Mrs Sword had set the class a difficult task – to work out how long it takes sunlight to travel to each of the planets in the solar system. It had seemed interesting at

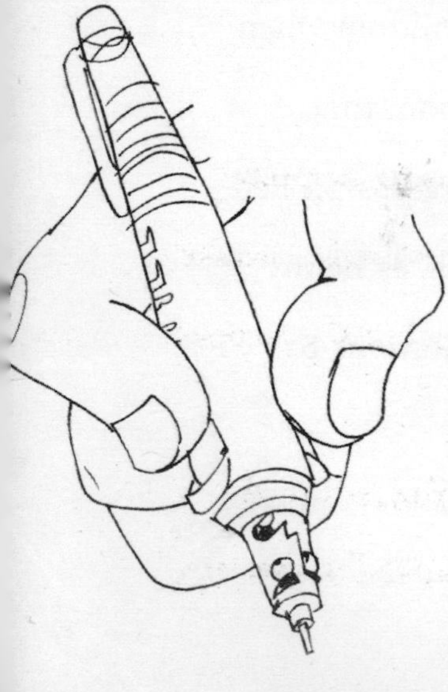

first, but once he had got into the exercise, Ralph realised it was just Mrs Sword's way of tricking the class into doing long division. Long division – and all maths for that matter – was not Ralph's strong point. He kept making mistakes and because the new space pen wrote in ink instead of pencil, he couldn't rub anything out. His page was so full of crossings out that it looked as though someone had spilled a big bottle of ink all over it.

Next to Ralph, Sarah was also using her anti-gravity space pen, but hadn't made a single mistake. Ralph peered over Sarah's shoulder, but she slapped her hand over her work.

'Honestly, Ralph,' said Sarah. 'If Mrs Sword catches you we'll both get into trouble for cheating.'

'But I just need some help getting started,' said Ralph.

Sarah looked at Ralph's ink-blotch covered page.

'If you're going to make that many mistakes you should be writing in pencil,' she whispered.

'Well I didn't know I was going to make so many mistakes before I started, did I?' grumbled Ralph, laying Sputink on the desk and pulling Penny out of his pencil case.

'Now all you have to do,' said Sarah, looking carefully in Mrs Sword's direction, 'is divide the distance of the planet from the sun by the speed of light. Just start off with Mercury, and once you get that right, move on to Venus. But not before I check it!'

'What planet are you up to?' asked Ralph.

'Saturn,' said Sarah. 'And it's my favourite planet so I'd really like to work this sum out.'

'Sorry,' said Ralph, going back to his own work.

Once Penny realised that Ralph's schoolwork was all about space, she stopped looking around the classroom and concentrated on the long division sum. Being a clever pencil, she'd worked out the answer long before Ralph had even written the equals sign.

Ralph did a page of working out, but got the answer wrong.

'Tch! That's what I got last time,' he said, dropping Penny on the desk next to Sputink and rummaging in his pencil case for Smudge.

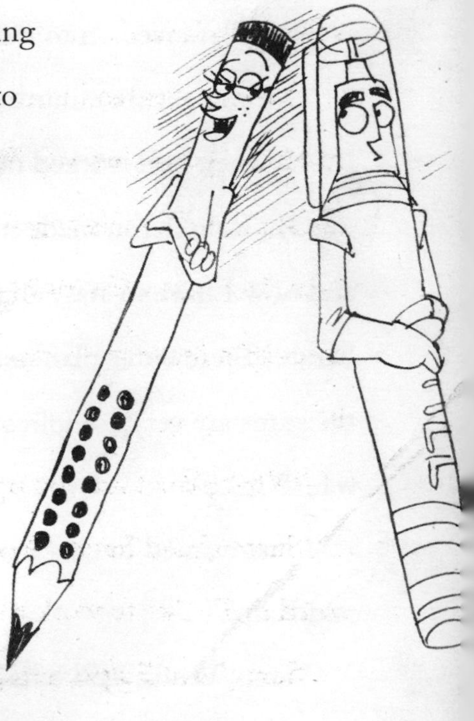

'Hey, Bleepy. How's it going?' asked Penny.

'Not all that great,' admitted Sputink. 'Somehow

the humanoid deactivated my retro jets and now I'm marooned on this dormant planet.'

'Aw, poor Sputink. If only I wasn't a lesser life-form, I might have the intelligence to help you,' said Penny, as Ralph dropped Smudge on the table and picked her up to write with again.

This time Ralph got the answer right, and having checked with Sarah (who was already up to Neptune!), moved on to the next planet, Venus.

'Did you get six minutes for Venus, Sarah?' asked Ralph when he'd worked out the answer.

'Oh, Ralph! You made me lose my concentration and now I have to start all over again,' huffed Sarah. 'These outer planets are very far away, so the sums are very complicated. Now what did you want?'

'I just wanted to check the answer for Venus,' said Ralph.

'Venus, Venus,' said Sarah, leafing through her

exercise book. 'That was pages ago. Did you get six minutes?'

'Yes!' said Ralph.

'Then either we're both right, or we're both wrong,' said Sarah, quickly checking her working out. 'Now you've got the hang of it, you don't have to check with me after every sum, okay?'

'Okay!' said Ralph, feeling quite pleased with himself.

It took Ralph the rest of the lesson to work out the sums for all the other planets. Sarah had finished with half the lesson to spare, so Mrs Sword had let her start on her rocket design early.

When Ralph got back to his desk after taking his maths book up to Mrs Sword's desk for correcting, he found Sarah and Bert having a heated argument. Sarah's rocket design had a huge streak across it and was totally ruined.

'You did it on purpose,' hissed Sarah.

'No I didn't,' said Bert nastily. 'It's not my fault your nerdy elbow sticks out when you draw.'

'My elbow's not nerdy and you crashed into me deliberately!' said Sarah.

The children were so busy shouting at each other they didn't notice the *click-clack* of Mrs Sword's shoes coming towards them.

'What's going on here?' demanded Mrs Sword.

'Bert bumped me and ruined my rocket design on purpose!' said Sarah.

'I didn't,' protested Bert. 'Her arm bumped me when I was walking past to bring up my maths book.'

Mrs Sword looked from Sarah to Bert, and then at Sarah's ruined rocket design.

'Well, there's no doubt that you'll have to start again with your rocket design, Sarah,' said Mrs Sword. 'But luckily you had a head start by finishing your planetary maths so quickly, so you haven't really lost anything.'

Sarah gaped at Mrs Sword.

'But he ...' she began.

'And as for you, Bert,' continued Mrs Sword. 'Maybe you'd like to come and sit in the first row, right in front of my desk, so that no one will bump into you next time you have something to hand in.'

Bert just looked at Mrs Sword.

'Come on,' said Mrs Sword. 'Gather up your books. You'll be sitting next to Malcolm from now on.'

Mrs Sword waited until Bert started collecting all his books together, then went back to her desk.

As Bert walked past Sarah he whispered, 'Don't think this is going to help you, Monaghan. You'll still have the worst rocket design in the class.'

'Leave her alone,' said Ralph.

'Make that the equal worst rocket design in the class,' said Bert, narrowing his eyes at Ralph and giving the desk an extra big bump for good measure on the way to his new seat at the front of the classroom.

Ralph and Sarah stared after him with narrowed eyes, while out on the desk, their pencils looked on in concern.

Chapter 5

Sputink Steps Up

Later that evening, after Ralph had finished his homework and gone to bed, Gloop called a special assembly of all the writing implements.

'What's this all about, Gloop?' asked Scarlet. As red was Ralph's favourite colour, the coloured pencils had elected Scarlet as their spokespencil.

'As you know, it's Space Week at school and Mrs Sword has set a big rocket design project,' said Gloop. 'No doubt all of us will play an important part in helping Ralph draw up his final design.'

Penny, Mack and Smudge looked on seriously as all the coloured pencils chattered excitedly to each other. Even Sputink, who had been looking down ever since Ralph had deactivated his retro jets, perked up immensely at the mention of the word 'rocket'.

'I'm sorry to spoil the festive mood,' continued Gloop, 'but it's come to my attention that Bert, and presumably certain members of his pencil case, may attempt to sabotage Ralph's design.'

All the pencils stopped their chattering and gasped.

'Why would Bert do that?' asked Amber.

'It's obvious, isn't it?' said Jade. 'Bert's always being nasty to Ralph and spoiling Ralph's work on a big project like this would be just the type of mean thing he'd do.'

'Precisely,' said Gloop. 'Which means we're going to have to be on special alert.'

'Do you have any idea how Bert will sabotage Ralph's project?' asked Scarlet.

'Most likely by scribbling over it when Ralph's not looking,' said Gloop.

'Like the time he got Black Texta to write all those nasty things on Ralph and Sarah's schoolwork?' asked Jade.

'Exactly,' said Gloop.

'Has … Black Texta … come back?' asked Rose, a pale pink pencil who went even paler at the mention of Black Texta.

'We don't have any evidence at all of Black Texta coming back,' said Gloop. 'As you know, Baron de Couberpen took care of him last time, shipping him off to boot camp in France.'

'But don't people come back from boot camp much stronger and braver?' asked Skye, the light blue pencil.

Gloop hesitated.

'And even after Penny set the lamp-beast on him that time, making him weaker, Black Texta still managed to come back and wreak havoc,' said Amber hysterically.

'Ladies, ladies, please don't panic,' said Gloop.

But it wasn't just the coloured pencils who were feeling anxious. Penny had gone a deathly shade of grey at the thought of the almost invincible Black Texta returning even more powerful than ever.

'As I said,' continued Gloop, over the worried chatter of the coloured pencils, 'we have no evidence whatsoever of Black Texta being back. This is something between Bert and Ralph, and we must be on our most vigilant to make sure nothing happens to Ralph's rocket design.'

Once the meeting had broken up, Gloop waddled over to Penny, Mack and Smudge.

'Well that didn't quite go to plan,' said Gloop. 'I tried to warn everyone to watch out for Bert, and those silly pencils have got themselves into a full-scale panic over Black Texta.'

'They're not the only ones,' said Penny, making Mack and Smudge start.

'What aren't you telling us, Penny?' asked Mack.

'It's nothing really,' said Penny. 'It's just a feeling I get whenever trouble's afoot and Black Texta's behind it.'

'But Penny,' said Gloop, 'like I told the assembly, Baron de Couberpen took Black Texta off to boot camp. In France!'

'But what if Skye's right?' said Penny. 'Just say Black Texta manages to escape, or gets discharged or whatever, and he comes back more evil and powerful than ever?'

'You're saying Black Texta and Bert just happen to be in this together,' said Gloop sarcastically.

'They usually are,' mumbled Penny.

'Come on,' said Gloop. 'Even if Black Texta were back, bent on revenge, he'd hardly be able to explain his plan to Bert, would he? Humans can't hear us when we talk.'

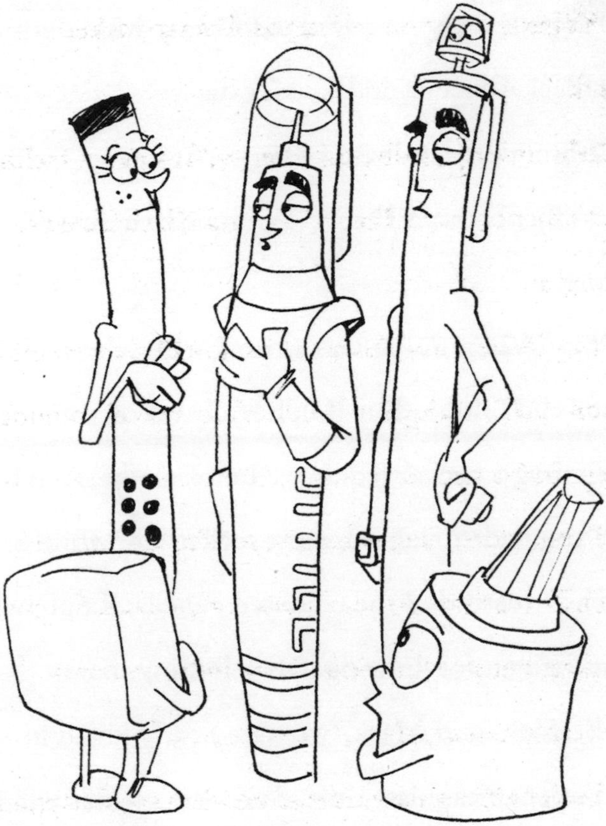

'Maybe Black Texta wrote the plan down,' suggested Smudge.

'Now you're assuming Bert can read,' snorted Mack.

'Gloop,' said Penny urgently, 'I've got to get into

Bert's pencil case and find out exactly what's going on, Black Texta or no Black Texta.'

'Absolutely not,' said Gloop.

'Why not?' said Penny. 'I've gone undercover before ...'

'Yes. When Ralph was writing with Mack all the time,' said Gloop. 'But Ralph really needs you now. Designing a rocket requires a lot of maths. And in case you hadn't realised, most rockets are white or silver, so instead of the coloured pencils, Ralph will be using you for drawing and colouring in.'

'Besides,' said Mack, 'we were nearly killed in Bert's pencil case last time. And Bert's textas will be on the look-out for you.'

'But they won't be on the look-out for me,' said a new voice.

Penny, Mack, Gloop and Smudge turned around to see Sputink hovering on the edge of their conversation.

'In fact, they'll be expecting me,' continued Sputink. 'Or rather someone who looks very much like me.'

Penny and the others looked at each other.

'All the children in the class got the same Space Week pack, didn't they?' said Sputink.

The others nodded.

'And all of those packs have a space pen that looks identical to me,' continued Sputink. 'All I have to do is lure Yuri out of Bert's pencil case, and go in there myself.'

'Who's Yuri?' asked Smudge.

'The space pen issued to Bert,' explained Sputink. 'Then, once I'm in there, I can report back to you about what's going on.'

'That's a great plan!' said Penny.

'With one drawback,' said Mack, who was still suspicious of the space pen. 'How will you know if Black Texta's in there?'

'I've seen a picture of a texta in the *Encyclopedia Universa*. I'll just look for a black one,' said Sputink.

'Was it also under L for lesser life-forms?' asked Mack.

'No. It was under E for evil species,' said Sputink.

The other four looked at each other hesitantly.

'Come on,' said Sputink. 'Ralph's hardly going to miss me. All I do is write the wrong thing and leave messy ink splotches all over the page. Plus, you'll have Yuri to replace me.'

'If you're sure …' said Gloop.

'Affirmative,' said Sputink. 'And I'll take extra precautions just in case Black Texta is more muscly and meaner than the picture in the encyclopedia.'

'Okay,' said Penny. 'The mission is yours.'

'There's just one thing,' said Sputink. 'I'll need my communicator back,' he said, putting his hand out towards Mack.

Grudgingly, Mack pulled the space age communicator off his own wrist and gave it to the space pen.

Chapter 6

The Evil Plan

Sputink got his chance to put his plan into action at school the next morning. After Ralph wowed the class during Show and Tell with a demonstration of his remote control Lunar Rover, Mrs Sword took the children out into the playground to teach them how to use a telescope to look at sunspots – which didn't involve looking through the telescope at all! – and all the pencil cases were left open on the desks.

Penny, Mack and Sputink snuck out of Ralph's pencil case and hid behind Ralph's Space Week book, where they had a clear view of Bert's desk

without being seen. When they were safely out of sight Sputink spoke into his communicator.

'Comrade Yuri, Comrade Yuri, this is Mission Control. Come in!'

Sputink pressed the 'receive' button, but only a hiss of static came through the communicator.

'Try again,' urged Penny.

'Comrade Yuri, Comrade Yuri. Come in! This is Mission Control. Do you read me?' said Sputink.

This time a voice replied, 'Mission Control, this is Yuri. I am receiving you. Over.'

'Comrade Yuri, we have a new assignment for you. It is imperative that you report to the desk of Comrade Sputink immediately, where you will receive new instructions. Over,' said Sputink.

'Affirmative. I will do so immediately. Over,' said Yuri, followed by a crackle of static.

A few moments later, bleeping could be heard overhead as Yuri flew out of Bert's pencil case and landed on Ralph's desk.

'Comrade Yuri reporting for duty,' said Yuri, saluting Sputink.

'You are relieved of your post,' said Sputink

harshly. 'You are to give me your communicator and retro jet pack immediately.'

'But why …?' began Yuri.

'Comrade! You are a member of the Space Corps elite. It is your duty to follow orders, not ask questions. Understood?' yelled Sputink in a voice so scary that Penny and Mack trembled a little.

'Yes, comrade,' said Yuri, taking off his retro jet pack and communicator.

Sputink put the retro jet pack on his own back and gave the communicator to Mack.

'I am leaving this pencil in charge,' said Sputink. 'Do as it says.'

And with that, Sputink fired up his retro jets and bleeped his way across the classroom to Bert's

pencil case. He got there just in time, as the sound of children's footsteps could be heard coming along the corridor.

'Quickly, inside!' said Mack, holding the zip open for Penny and Yuri to slip inside Ralph's pencil case.

The classroom door opened and the children filed into the room, followed by Mrs Sword. Once everyone was seated, Mrs Sword said, 'How did you enjoy that?'

The children all started talking at once.

'One at a time!' said Mrs Sword.

Lucy put up her hand.

'Yes, Lucy,' said Mrs Sword.

'Why did we have to put a piece of paper behind the telescope to look at sunspots instead of looking through the telescope?' asked Lucy.

'Because looking at the sun is very bad for your eyes,' said Mrs Sword, 'and since the telescope makes things bigger it would be much, much worse and you'd go blind!'

The children gasped, glad that none of them had accidentally looked through the telescope.

'Now,' continued Mrs Sword, handing out some papers, 'I have permission slips for you to take home and have your parents sign so that you can attend our special observation night on Thursday evening.'

'What's an observation night?' asked Seán.

'It's when you come to school after dark to look through the telescope at the moon and some stars and planets,' explained Mrs Sword.

'Oh, wow!' said Sarah excitedly. 'I love Space Week! I hope we get to do it again.'

Meanwhile, inside Bert's pencil case, Sputink was flying around looking for Black Texta. As he

orbited towards the deepest, darkest corner of the pencil case, he saw the unmistakable shape of a big, black, mean-looking texta. Bleeping as quietly as he could, Sputink turned on his communicator and flew in as close as he dared.

*

In a neighbouring pencil case, Penny, Mack, Smudge and Gloop were gathered around Yuri's communicator. When Sputink started broadcasting there was a hiss of static, followed by the unmistakable sound of Black Texta's voice.

'That's excellent news, Cheetah,' they heard Black Texta say. 'Now here's how we are to proceed. We have to leave it until the last possible moment, when there is the least chance of recovery. If we strike too soon, Ralph and Sarah may be able to redraw their designs. But if we scribble all over them on Thursday night while the children are in the playground observing, well! Our plan won't be discovered until

Friday, when it will be too late for Ralph and Sarah to redo their designs.'

Black Texta laughed one of his evil laughs that made Penny tremble from head to toe, even though she was the other side of the classroom from her arch enemy.

'Did you hear that?' said Smudge. 'That evil texta's going to wreck both Ralph and Sarah's rocket designs. We've got to stop him!'

'And we've got to warn Sarah's pencils,' said Penny.

'At least we have some time to prepare,' said Gloop. 'We have until Thursday night to think of a good counter-plan.'

The lunch bell rang and Penny made her way to the zip.

'I'll just wait until the children leave, then I'll quickly pop over to Sarah's pencil case to fetch Polly. The more heads we have working on this, the better!' said Penny.

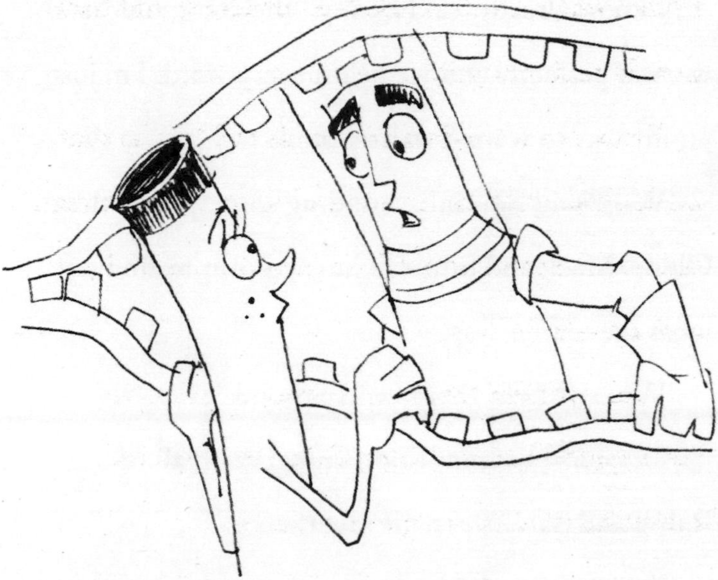

She waited until the sound of the last child's footsteps had disappeared and opened the zip. But instead of having a clear run across the desk to Sarah's pencil case, Penny found her way blocked by Sputink trying to come in.

'What are you doing back here?' Penny asked.

'It's … bleep … worse than we … bleep … thought,' said Sputink, touching down just inside the zip.

'I know already,' said Penny. 'The communicator worked perfectly and we heard every word. I'm just on my way to warn Sarah's pencils …'

'Wait!' said Sputink, sounding so desperate that Gloop, Mack and Smudge hurried over to find out what the matter was.

'We can't fight them,' said Sputink.

'Of course we can,' said Penny. 'With all of Ralph and Sarah's pencils together …'

'No!' said Sputink.

Penny's eyes opened wide in alarm.

'Even all the pencils in all the pencil cases belonging to all the children in the classroom put together couldn't fight them off,' said Sputink.

'Them?' said Mack.

'It's not just Black Texta who's been to boot camp,' said Sputink. 'His entire texta army is looking meaner and more muscly than anything I've ever seen in the *Encyclopedia Universa*, and there are some truly frightening species in there. They'd crush us in seconds!'

'Are you saying that there's nothing we can do?' said Gloop.

'We can't fight them,' said Sputink, shaking his head sadly.

'Then we'll just have to outsmart them,' said Penny, the beginnings of a smile pulling at the corners of her mouth. 'And I know just how to do it!'

Chapter 7

Lunar Orbiter

When the bell rang for home time, instead of rushing out with the other children, Ralph and Sarah stayed behind in the classroom, looking for something.

'Why didn't you put it straight back in your bag after Show and Tell?' asked Sarah from behind the drawers.

'I'm sure I did,' said Ralph's muffled voice from inside the cupboard under the blackboard.

'Could you have put it in someone else's bag by mistake? Ow!' said Sarah, accidentally slamming a drawer shut on her fingers.

Ralph waved the remote control over his head and said, 'I'd have to be pretty stupid to put the remote control in one bag and the Rover in the other, wouldn't I?'

Sarah stayed silent for a moment.

'Hey – I have an idea!' she said, smiling. 'Why don't you turn the remote control on and make the Lunar Rover drive back to us?'

'That's a great idea!' said Ralph sarcastically.

'Now if only I knew where the Rover was, I'd know what direction to steer it in.'

'Hmmm,' said Sarah, furrowing her brow. 'Why not make it drive round in circles? We might be able to hear the engine, or at least hear a bang if it crashes into something.'

'That's more like it!' said Ralph, turning on the remote control and using the joystick to make the Rover drive around in a circle.

But as much as they strained their ears, Ralph and Sarah heard nothing.

Ralph let out a sigh.

'It's no use. It's gone for good,' he said.

'Maybe not,' said Sarah, resuming her search. 'Maybe the batteries are flat, or it's jammed in somewhere and can't move, or the signal can't get to it because it's in a Faraday cage ...'

'What's a Faraday?' asked Ralph, looking in the guinea pig cage.

'Never mind,' said Sarah.

The *click-clack* of a pair of high heels stopped Ralph and Sarah mid conversation.

'What are you two still doing here?' asked Mrs Sword.

'We're looking for Ralph's Lunar Rover,' said Sarah. 'It's gone missing.'

'Tsk,' tsked Mrs Sword. 'You should have given it to me to mind, Ralph.'

'I know,' said Ralph in a small voice.

'I'll help you look for five minutes,' said Mrs Sword, 'but after that you're to go straight home, otherwise your mother and grandmother will think something's happened to you.'

But it was no use. Even with the three of them scouring the entire classroom, the Lunar Rover was not to be found.

'Cheer up, Ralph,' said Sarah as they walked home. 'Your birthday's coming up soon. Maybe you can ask your mum for a new one.'

'Maybe,' said Ralph, knowing how disappointed his mother would be when he told her he'd lost something very expensive.

Ralph flicked idly with the remote control. Sarah held her tongue, knowing it was best to say nothing to Ralph when he was in one of those moods. When they got to the park, Sarah thought she could hear a whirring sound.

'Stop,' she said, grabbing Ralph by the arm.

Ralph stood still and stopped playing with the remote control.

'Do something with the remote,' whispered Sarah.

Ralph tilted the joystick that made the Rover go forward. A very faint whirring could be heard coming from behind a tree in the park.

'Can you hear that?' whispered Sarah.

'It's the Rover!' said Ralph, running towards the tree.

Sarah took off after him. As they rounded the tree, they saw the Lunar Rover on its back, with what looked like a firework strapped to the top. And standing just behind the Lunar Rover was Bert.

'Step right up, step right up, ladies and gentlemen!' said Bert, like a ringmaster at the circus. 'Today we will see the amazing transformation from Lunar Rover to Lunar Orbiter. Silence if you please.'

'What are you doing with my Lunar Rover?' demanded Ralph.

'Letting it fulfil its purpose and making it fly to the moon,' said Bert, striking a match.

'No!' yelled Ralph, running towards the Rover, but Sarah held him back.

'Ralph! Don't you know what that is? It's too dangerous!'

Bert held the match to a fuse on the end of the firework. He took one step back and held his hands over his ears.

The flame raced up the shortening fuse towards the firework, and there was an almighty *bang*! The firework and Lunar Rover shot into the air.

'Woohoo!' yelled Bert. 'Look at it fly!'

Ralph watched on in horror as the Rover flew away from them.

'And three ... two ... one ...' said Bert.

The firework exploded with a shower of red and yellow sparks, tearing the Lunar Rover apart.

'Duck!' cried Sarah, as pieces of what used to be Lunar Rover rained down upon them.

When Ralph and Sarah looked up again, Bert was jumping up and down with glee.

'I guess it's all over for your Rover,' laughed Bert.

'Why you ...' began Ralph, heading towards Bert with his fist clenched.

'Hey,' said Sarah, holding Ralph back again.

'You're not that tough, Ralphee, if you can be held back by a girl,' taunted Bert.

'Toughness has nothing to do with it,' said Sarah. 'I just thought that Ralph shouldn't punch the boy who's going to buy him a new Lunar Rover.'

'That's no one around here,' sneered Bert.

'Wanna bet?' said Sarah, pulling a handkerchief out of her pocket and picking up a smouldering

piece of Rover debris. 'Fireworks are illegal. If I take this to the police, and tell them what you did, they'll be able to match your fingerprints and you'll go to juvenile detention.'

Bert's sneer weakened a little.

'Really?' he said doubtfully.

'Have you ever known me to be wrong?' asked Sarah.

'Fine,' said Bert, 'I'll buy Ralph a new Lunar Rover and bring it to school tomorrow.'

'You'd better,' said Sarah, 'or I'm taking this straight to the police!'

Ralph and Sarah watched as Bert stalked off.

'Uh, Bert,' called Sarah. 'The toy shop's that way.'

'I know,' said Bert. 'But I have to go home and steal – I mean borrow – some money from Mum's purse first.'

Once Bert was out of sight, Ralph turned to his best friend and gave her a big hug.

'That was brilliant!' he said. 'How did you know the police could do that?'

'Only by watching our favourite TV show, *Officer Cool*!' said Sarah, looking at her watch. 'And it's about to start in five minutes. Let's go!'

Chapter 8

A Stellar Opportunity

True to his word, Bert brought Ralph's new Lunar Rover to school the next day, and grudgingly exchanged it for the piece of evidence Sarah had collected from the illegal launch. Ralph gave the Rover straight to Mrs Sword for safe-keeping, so he was able to concentrate properly on learning about space and designing his own rocket, which – unlike Bert's – would not destroy its payload moments after take-off.

On Thursday evening Ralph, Sarah and even Bert were having a wonderful time looking at the moon and planets and a couple of galaxies through

the telescope in the playground, unaware of the frenzied activity going on in the classroom. Penny and Polly were leading Ralph and Sarah's pencils in their counter-plan, feverishly trying to put the final preparations in place before Black Texta launched his attack.

'Hurry!' cried Penny. 'If Black Texta sees us, it'll all be for nothing.'

'We're doing the best we can,' cried Ralph and Sarah's coloured pencils.

Suddenly there was a warning bark. Smudge, who was on pencil case patrol, noticed the zipper of Bert's pencil case start to jiggle as though someone was trying to open it from the inside.

'He's coming!' cried Penny. 'Everyone back inside the pencil cases. Hurry!'

Penny made sure everyone was safely inside Ralph and Sarah's pencil cases before going through the zip herself. But it was too late. A black hand grabbed her shoulder in a vice-like grip, pulling her away from the pencil case and flinging her to the other side of the desk.

Penny lay dazed as a large, black writing implement advanced upon her.

'Ms Penny Pencil. What brings you outside your pencil case on this fine, moonlit evening?' said the threatening voice of Black Texta.

Looking up at him, Penny could hardly believe her eyes. Black Texta had nearly doubled in size, and his huge muscles were threatening to burst out of his plastic casing. Sputink had been right – not even all the pencils in the classroom put together could have stood up to this new Black Texta.

'I see you're back from boot camp,' said Penny.

'Yes,' said Black Texta. 'It was more of a holiday than

a punishment. I should really thank Baron de Couberpen for sending me there.'

'If boot camp suited you so well, why did you leave?' asked Penny.

'One word,' said Black Texta. 'The one word that got me through boot camp: all those five a.m. starts, the gruelling workouts, the dreadful French cuisine – can you imagine being force-fed garlic snails for breakfast! Do you want to know what that word is, Penny Pencil?'

'I guess you're going to tell me regardless …'

'REVENGE!' boomed Black Texta. 'Revenge against the one being who keeps foiling all my plans, turning my texta army against me, making me look like a fool. Revenge. Against YOU!'

It took all of Penny's willpower not to start shaking.

'Are you going to kill me?' asked Penny in a small voice.

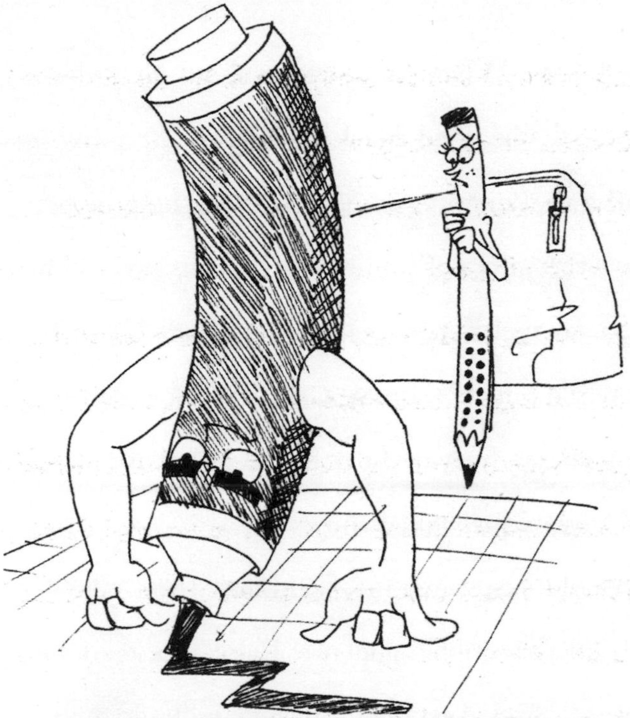

‘Oh, no,’ said Black Texta quietly. ‘At boot camp I learned that there are worse fates than death. Rather than killing you, I am going to destroy the one thing you care about more than anything else in the world – Ralph!’

This time, Penny couldn’t hide her fear.

‘You … you’re going to k-kill Ralph?’ stammered Penny.

'Kill him? What did I just say about fates worse than death?' laughed Black Texta. 'I'm not going to kill him. I'm going to destroy everything he does. Every piece of homework he hands in will be ruined. By me! Every spelling test, spoiled. By me! And while I'm at it, I may as well wreck everything that little goody-two-shoes friend of his does too!'

'You wouldn't!' said Penny.

'I would! Just watch me,' said Black Texta, taking off his lid and scribbling all over Ralph's rocket design.

When Black Texta had finished, he looked up at Penny and smirked, before rolling over to Sarah's desk and scribbling all over her design too.

'That should pretty much do it,' said Black Texta, smiling smugly.

He put his lid back on, and went back to Bert's pencil case, laughing his evil laugh all the way.

'It's too late to fix it now, but break a lead trying!' he called, just before disappearing through the zip.

Penny stayed put on the desk until Bert's zip was fully closed, then got up and whistled.

Mack, Smudge and some of Sarah's pencils came out of their pencil cases.

'Did he fall for it?' asked Polly.

'Hook, line and sinker,' said Penny, smiling and crumpling up Ralph's old rocket design. 'Let's throw these in the rubbish!'

When Sarah and Ralph got to their desks the next morning they stopped short. Their rocket designs, which they'd left on top of their desks, were missing. Sarah looked on top of the desk, inside it, on her chair and even on the floor, but there was no sign of her design anywhere.

'My rocket design's missing,' said Sarah.

'So's mine,' said Ralph.

From the front of the classroom, Bert sniggered.

'Bert!' said Sarah, looking up sharply. 'What have you done with our rocket designs?'

'Don't look at me,' said Bert, spreading his arms wide and smirking.

'Good morning, class!' said Mrs Sword. 'If you'd all bring your rocket designs up to my desk, I'll pin them on the board while you do your planetary maths exercise. Ah, Ralph and Sarah, I see you've already handed yours in.'

Ralph and Sarah looked at each other.

'I don't remember doing that,' said Sarah. 'Did you ...?'

'No,' said Ralph. 'I thought you must have ...'

Sarah was so busy keeping one eye on Mrs Sword as she hung up the drawings, that for the first time ever Ralph finished his sums before her.

'They're definitely our rocket designs,' said Sarah, 'but how did they get up to Mrs Sword's desk all on their own?'

'Who cares? The important thing is that they're not lost, and even more importantly, I finished before you!' said Ralph, holding his completed sums in front of Sarah's nose.

Just as Mrs Sword had finished pinning up the last drawing, there was a knock at the classroom door.

'That's probably our special guest,' said Mrs Sword. 'Pencils down everybody.'

All the children put their pencils down and sat up very straight as Mrs Sword opened the door. In walked a very tall lady in a flight suit.

'Class, say hello to our special guest, Ms Stella Nebula,' said Mrs Sword.

'Good morning, Ms Nebula,' said the children.

'Good morning, budding astronauts,' said Ms Nebula.

'Are you a real astronaut?' asked Malcolm.

'Yes I am,' said Ms Nebula. 'I work for NOSA, the National Orbiting Satellite Association.'

'How did you get to be an astronaut?' asked Sarah.

'I studied really hard at school, doing lots of Maths and Physics,' said Ms Nebula.

'What's Physics?' asked Ciara.

'The study of forces and the way things move, and how the universe fits together,' said Ms Nebula. 'Plus, astronauts have to be really fit, so I spent almost as much time exercising as studying.'

'Have you been into space?' asked Seán.

'Seven times,' said Ms Nebula. 'And I've done five space walks.'

The class had learned all about space walks during the week, and were very impressed that Ms Nebula had been outside her space ship wearing only a space suit.

'Now, I understand that you've been busy designing your own rockets,' said Ms Nebula.

'Yes,' said Mrs Sword. 'They've all worked very hard and the final designs are pinned up on the board.'

Ms Nebula went to the board and looked at the designs carefully.

'These are all very good,' she said. 'And this one has an amazing propulsion design,' she commented, when she got to Bert's. 'Mrs Sword, could I have a word?'

Mrs Sword walked over to Ms Nebula and they whispered quietly between themselves for a few moments before turning back to the class.

'Ms Nebula is so impressed with your projects that she has a special announcement to make!' said Mrs Sword.

The whole class drew in their breaths, and Ralph and Sarah's pencils peered out of their pencil cases excitedly.

'Every year at NOSA we run a special Space Camp for budding astronauts,' began Ms Nebula. 'And by the quality of your project work I can see this is a class full of budding astronauts.'

All the children beamed at each other proudly.

'That's the good news,' said Ms Nebula. 'The bad news is that our Space Camp is very popular, and we only have three places left.'

Some of the children's faces fell, but most of the class remained hopeful that they might be one of the lucky three to get to go to Space Camp.

'The following three names are the children I have chosen to come to Space Camp, based on the outstanding work displayed in their rocket designs,' continued Ms Nebula. 'Those three budding Space Campers are, in no particular order: Sarah!'

Everyone clapped for Sarah and Ralph patted her on the back saying, 'Well done! You're going to Space Camp!'

On the desk below them, Sarah's pencil case wiggled about with all the pencils dancing inside.

'The next Space Camper,' continued Ms Nebula, 'is Ralph!'

The class burst into applause again, and Sarah nudged Ralph saying, 'We're going to Space Camp together!'

They were so excited neither of them noticed Ralph's pencil case wobbling around even more than Sarah's as Penny and her friends celebrated.

'And the lucky last Space Camper,' said Ms Nebula as the entire class held their breath for their final chance to go to Space Camp, 'is Bert!'

Bert leapt up out of his seat and shouted, 'No school for a week! Woohoo!'

'That's not quite the attitude I was hoping for,'

said Ms Nebula, 'but congratulations to all the winners. I'll see you at Space Camp next week. And don't forget to bring your rocket designs with you. Have a good weekend.'

Chapter 9

Ethelbert

The following Monday morning, Penny and all of Ralph's pencils, including Gloop and Smudge, were awake and eager for the first day of Space Camp.

'Space Camp!' said Amber excitedly. 'Do you think it'll be full of good-looking astronaut pens?'

'I hope so,' said Jade, looking jealously over to where Rose and Scarlet were having breakfast with Sputink and Yuri. 'Two just isn't enough to go round!'

'I bet the Space Camp instructors are even stronger and better-looking than those two freebies,' said Amber.

'Yeah,' agreed Jade. 'I'd say Space Camp really separates the pen from the toys!'

And with that, both the gossipy pencils erupted into a fit of giggles.

'Do you think Ralph and Sarah will build real rockets, and we'll get to go on a real rocket ride?' Penny asked Mack.

'Now, now, Penny,' said Gloop before Mack

had a chance to answer, 'you remember what Stella Nebula said about becoming an astronaut. It takes years of study and physical training, and I dare say the same goes for the astronauts' writing implements.'

'Why are you always such a spoil-sport?' demanded Penny. 'Whenever I get excited about something, you say it takes years of study …'

'Well I don't want you getting your hopes up too high …' began Gloop.

'But that's the whole point of Space Camp, isn't it?' said Penny. 'The sky is no longer the limit.'

'Seriously,' said Mack, unused to being the peacemaker, 'it might not be all fun and games. Bert's also going to Space Camp, which means you know who will probably be there too.'

'And he'll be doing everything he can to make sure that if any of us do make it into space, it'll be a one-way trip,' said Smudge.

Before the pencils could say anything further, the walls of the pencil case started to close in on them.

'This is it!' said Penny, momentarily forgetting the threat of Black Texta. 'Ralph's putting us in his backpack and taking us to Space Camp!'

*

'Hurry up, Ralph!' called his mother from the driveway. 'I promised Sarah's grandmother we'd be at her house five minutes ago. And we also have to pick up Bert.'

'Don't remind me,' muttered Ralph, stuffing his pyjamas into his backpack and running downstairs.

'There's my little astronaut,' said Ralph's mother, ruffling his hair as he got in the car. 'Now you've packed enough pairs of undies?'

'Yes, Mum,' said Ralph, glad that Sarah and Bert weren't yet in the car with his mother talking about underwear.

'Enough handkerchiefs?'

'Yes.'

'Singlets?'

'As many as I need,' said Ralph, who hated wearing singlets and never thought he needed one.

Luckily Ralph was spared further interrogation as they had arrived at Sarah's.

Sarah and her grandmother were standing on the doorstep. Sarah was carrying her backpack, and her grandmother was holding something that looked suspiciously like a cake container.

'Now, I've baked you a cake to share, just in case the food at Space Camp isn't up to scratch,' said Sarah's grandmother. 'But you can only eat it on

the condition that you at least try to eat all your vegetables first.'

'We promise, Granny,' said Sarah.

'All right then, enjoy yourselves now!' waved Sarah's grandmother as Ralph's mother drove them off to pick up Bert.

They pulled up outside Bert's house and tooted the horn. There was no sign of Bert.

'I wonder where he is?' said Ralph's mother.

'Can't we just go on without him?' suggested Ralph.

'Ralph! That's not very nice,' said his mother.

'Bert's not very nice,' mumbled Ralph.

'Run up and knock on the door,' said Ralph's mother.

'Do I have to? Why don't you toot again?' asked Ralph.

'Because I don't want to annoy the neighbours,' said his mother.

Ralph sat in the back with his arms crossed.

'Ralph, if you don't go and knock on the door, I won't drive you to Space Camp either!'

Reluctantly, Ralph unbuckled his seatbelt and slammed the door as he got out of the car. He stomped up the front path and rang the bell.

Bert opened the door immediately, as though he'd been waiting there all along.

'Good of you to offer to carry my bag,' said Bert, shoving his backpack into Ralph's stomach and sauntering off towards the car.

Ralph let the bag fall to the ground with a loud thud making Bert turn around.

'What's the problem?' said Bert. 'Too heavy for you?'

'You want it,' said Ralph, 'you carry it yourself.'

And before Bert could say another word, Ralph

had run past him and hopped into the back seat of the car, next to Sarah and the cake.

Bert put his bag in the boot and opened the door next to Sarah.

'Shove over, Monaghan,' he said nastily.

'Bert, you can sit up front here with me,' said Ralph's mother who had watched the bully's performance angrily and finally understood why the children didn't like Bert.

'Why does he get to sit in the front?' complained Ralph as Bert slammed the back door.

'Because I won't have him in the back annoying you two,' said Ralph's mother quickly, before Bert had opened the front door.

Although they had started the morning running a little late, they arrived at Space Camp right on time. Ralph's mum drove up to a big gate with NOSA written on it. A soldier came out of a patrol box next to the gate and asked Ralph's mum for her name.

‘I’m Sandra Nolan,’ said Ralph’s mother. ‘I’m dropping my son and his friends off at Space Camp.’

‘Would that be Ralph Nolan?’ asked the soldier, reading through a list of names.

‘That’s me,’ said Ralph.

‘What’s your name, young lady?’ the soldier asked Sarah.

‘Sarah Monaghan,’ said Sarah, watching the soldier tick her name off his list.

‘I’m Bert O’Leary,’ said Bert.

'O'Leary, O'Leary …' said the soldier, looking through the list. 'Is Bert short for something?'

'Er …' said Bert, turning bright red.

'We don't have a Bert O'Leary,' continued the soldier, 'but we do have an Ethelbert.'

'That's me,' said Bert in a small voice as Ralph and Sarah cupped their hands over their mouths to hide their giggling.

The soldier ticked Bert's name off the list and turned back to Ralph's mother.

'Madam, as this is a military facility and your name isn't on the list, I can't let you through the gate. You kids'll have to go on foot from here. Okay?'

Everyone got out of the car, and the children grabbed their bags from the boot.

'Have a good time,' said Ralph's mother, giving him a hug and kiss in front of the soldier. 'You too, Sarah. And you, Ethelbert!'

Bert pulled a face and stalked off ahead of Ralph and Sarah who didn't even try to hide their laughter.

Chapter 10

Welcome to Space Camp

Still giggling, Ralph and Sarah followed Bert at a safe distance along the main path. They soon came to a lawn which had rows of chairs facing a stage. Lots of children their age were sitting in the chairs, talking to each other excitedly.

Ralph and Sarah chose their seats as far away from Bert as possible, sitting next to a little girl with glasses.

'Hi, I'm Aisling,' said the girl as they sat down.

'I'm Sarah, and this is Ralph,' said Sarah.

More and more children arrived, all of them saying hello or waving at Aisling as they sat down.

'Are you famous?' asked Sarah.

'Only in some circles,' said Aisling, blushing.

'How do you know everyone?' asked Ralph.

'We see each other at these things all the time,' said Aisling, waving to a pair of twin boys. 'Maths Camp, Chemistry Camp, Trigonometry Camp … Is this your first enlightened learner experience?'

'Er, yes,' said Sarah, realising that for the first time in her life she may not be the brightest child in the class.

'Well, just remember, you have as much right to be here as everyone else, and don't let anyone intimidate you,' advised Aisling.

'Ais!' cried a girl with pig-tails and make-up, leaning over Ralph and Sarah to give Aisling a hug.

'Hi Hunni,' said Aisling, less than enthusiastically.

'Who are your new friends?' said Hunni, looking down her nose at Ralph and Sarah.

'This is Sarah and Ralph,' said Aisling. 'It's their first camp.'

'Really?' said Hunni. 'What did you do to get here? Win a ticket?'

'No,' said Sarah. 'We did really well on our rocket design projects.'

'Did you now?' said Hunni. 'You must be budding astrophysicists then. Tell me, what's your opinion on Fluke's use of the ray bundle method in gravitational lensing?'

'I ... um ... don't really have an opinion ...' said Sarah, not understanding a word Hunni had said.

'Thought not,' said Hunni, flouncing off to sit with some other students.

'Don't mind her,' said Aisling. 'She's still upset at coming second in the hydrogen fuel cell competition at Environment Camp.'

'Who came first?' asked Ralph.

'Er, I did,' admitted Aisling, blushing deeply.

Aisling was saved from further embarrassment by a loud 'Good morning!'

Stella Nebula was standing on the stage, dressed in her flight suit, next to four other grown-ups, also wearing flight suits.

'Welcome to Space Camp. It's wonderful to see

so many future astronauts and aerospace engineers here at NOSA.

'Our special project this week is to build rockets we'll send up into space. But of course that's not all we'll be doing. While you're at NOSA you'll be living like real NOSA astronauts and engineers. You'll be wearing the NOSA uniform, doing

NOSA astronaut training and learning what it's like to be part of the NOSA team. Of course, we expect you to behave like NOSA staff, keeping yourselves and your quarters spic and span and putting 100 per cent into everything you do. Any questions so far?' asked Stella Nebula, looking around the rows of children.

Ralph was tempted to put up his hand and ask Ms Nebula if she'd made a mistake in choosing him to come to Space Camp, but he kept quiet.

'Let me introduce you to your NOSA instructors for the week. In charge of Flight Training we have Captain Saul R. Flare.'

Captain Flare stepped forward and saluted to the children.

'Teaching Planetary Science we have Professor Ursula Major.'

Professor Major stepped forward and gave an identical salute to Captain Flare.

'Specialising in Astral Navigation we have Lieutenant Con Stellation.'

Lieutenant Stellation stepped forward with the same salute.

'And for Advanced Relativity, specialising in the twin paradox, is Doctor Gemma Nigh.'

Dr Nigh stepped forward and saluted, just as the others had done.

'I will, of course, be teaching you Aerospace Engineering and supervising your construction projects,' continued Ms Nebula. 'But before we get too involved with lessons, we'll show you to your quarters where you can drop off your bags and change into your Space Camp uniforms. Girls, come with me. Boys, follow Captain Flare.'

Ralph watched Sarah and Aisling disappear with the rest of the girls before catching up with the boys. Bert was at the back of the line, waiting for Ralph, and looking suspiciously friendly.

'Have you ever seen such a bunch of nerds?' said Bert as Ralph reluctantly caught up to him. 'These guys think it's cool to spend their summer holidays going to Calculus Camp. I don't even know what calculus is, but it sounds geeky.'

A few of the boys ahead of them turned around with interest at the mention of the word 'calculus'.

'Why are you telling me this?' asked Ralph quietly.

'Never thought I'd say this,' said Bert, clapping Ralph on the shoulder, 'but you and me are the coolest dudes here. Even Monaghan looks normal compared to these freaks.'

The boys who had been listening in to their conversation narrowed their eyes when Bert called them freaks.

'Didn't your mother ever tell you that if you can't say anything nice, don't say anything at all?' hissed Ralph.

'Like I'd ever listen to her!' said Bert.

'Well I've had enough of listening to you!' said Ralph, walking quickly ahead until there were several boys between himself and Bert.

'Here we are,' said Captain Flare when they reached the boys' dormitory. 'Your names are on your bunks. You have exactly five minutes to change into your flight suits. Let's reconvene out here at zero-nine-twenty hours sharp. Anyone who's late will be on latrine duty.'

Keen to avoid latrine duty, the boys poured into

the dormitory. Ralph found his name on the top bed of the second bunk. He was relieved to see Bert keep walking all the way to the far end of the dormitory.

Ralph put his backpack in his locker and quickly changed into his uniform. It was a flight suit, just like the ones the instructors wore, with a cloth badge saying 'Ralph' sewn across the front pocket.

'Hi Ralph, I'm Colin,' said a boy with 'Colin' sewn across his pocket. 'We're bunk buddies. I hope you don't snore. My bunk buddy at Physics Camp was a terrible snorer.'

'I've never heard myself snore,' said Ralph, 'but then I've always been asleep at the time.'

Colin burst out laughing.

'You're funny,' he said, throwing an arm around Ralph's shoulders as they walked outside to reconvene with Captain Flare. 'I can tell we're going to be friends.'

*

Once all the boys had left the dormitory, Penny wriggled out of the pencil case and peered out through the grill at the bottom of Ralph's locker.

'What do you see?' asked Smudge.

'Just two rows of bunks, with lockers in between,' said Penny.

'You mean we're not even in a classroom?' said Mack.

'Afraid not,' said Penny.

'What else can you see?' asked Sputink.

'Nothing,' said Penny.

'Nothing?' said Mack. 'What sort of enlightened

learner experience is this if the children don't have to write anything down?'

'Maybe they've been issued new pens,' suggested Yuri.

'Why would they need new pens when there's a perfectly good pencil case full of ...' Penny trailed off, looking at Sputink and Yuri floating above the other pencils and bleeping quietly.

'Ah,' she said.

'Don't jump to any conclusions,' said Gloop. 'If the children are doing astronaut training, they probably don't need their pencils right now.'

'Hmmm,' said Penny, all the excitement of Space Camp draining away.

'And look on the bright side,' said Smudge. 'If Black Texta's locked away in a locker, he's less likely to do any damage to Ralph.'

'Ngh,' nghed Penny, tapping the steel of the locker door with her toe, knowing it was going to take a lot more than astronaut training and a flimsy steel door to hold Black Texta back.

'Now why don't we go back inside the pencil case and rest?' suggested Gloop. 'I was listening to Ms Nebula's welcome speech this morning, and the subjects they are studying sound hard. When Ralph does sit down to write with us we're going to need to be in top condition.'

With a final glance through the grill to make sure Black Texta hadn't already escaped from Bert's locker, Penny went and joined her friends back in the pencil case.

Chapter 11

Orientation

The boys and girls met up again outside a very tall building. It was made entirely of white painted metal, and had no windows at all. A widely-spaced train track ran right up to one of the walls of the building and disappeared inside.

'This is the NOSA rocket hangar,' said Captain Flare. 'This is where we build the rockets to launch the NOSA satellites into space. As you can see, the building is thirty storeys tall. That's the height of our tallest rockets.'

'Wow,' said Ralph and Sarah, even though everyone else didn't seem to think this was an amazing new fact.

'The rockets you will be building won't need to be anywhere near this tall,' said Ms Nebula. 'Remember, you only have one week to build your rockets, and it takes a team of 100 people four months to build one of these.'

'Does that mean you only launch three new satellites each year?' asked Hunni, smiling like someone who already knew the answer and was just showing off.

'Not at all,' said Captain Flare. 'We can actually take several satellites up per launch, and sometimes we just send our astronauts – like Ms Nebula here – up to repair or upgrade existing satellites.'

Hunni's smirk quickly disappeared.

'What are the train tracks for?' asked Ralph.

'Well-spotted,' said Captain Flare. 'These are for moving the rockets from the hangar to the launch pad, which is way over there.'

Captain Flare pointed along the train tracks that disappeared into the distance.

'Now who'd like to go inside and watch a real rocket being built?'

'Me!' said all the children excitedly.

'This is a construction zone, so you'll have to put hardhats on and keep them on the whole time you're inside,' said Ms Nebula, handing each child a hat as they went through the door into the hangar.

It was very noisy inside. People in white overalls were drilling and hammering away at the nearly finished rocket. The rocket itself seemed to tower up forever. When Ralph and Sarah stood at its base, the tip of it seemed to disappear into the roof.

'The launch is scheduled for Friday afternoon,' yelled Captain Flare over the noise of the busy workers. 'You'll all have time off classes to come and watch it. Let's move on to Mission Control.'

Captain Flare led the children out a door where Ms Nebula was waiting to collect their hardhats. The Mission Control building was much smaller than the rocket hangar. The children filed in one after the other, and even the seasoned enlightened learners couldn't hide their amazement. There were rows and rows of people sitting at computer terminals, all facing a large screen that took up the entire front wall. It showed a map of the Earth, with the position of every single NOSA satellite marked on it.

'What are all the people doing?' asked Aisling.

'They're monitoring the satellites to make sure they're sending and receiving data correctly and not floating off-course,' said Captain Flare.

'Why don't they just have one computer that controls everything?' asked Colin.

'Because people are still smarter than computers,' said Captain Flare. 'Any other questions? No? Then let's leave the satellite operators to their work and press on.'

Captain Flare led the children to the next building. Inside it smelled of chlorine and sweat.

'This is the Fitness Centre,' said Captain Flare. 'NOSA astronauts do a minimum of two hours each day in the gym, lifting weights, swimming, doing aerobics, cycling and running. When they're coming up to a mission, their exercise time increases to at least four hours a day. During Space Camp, you'll also be spending some time in here as part of your flight training programme.'

They walked past the gym equipment and down a narrow corridor. At the end was a group of doors, each with a red light overhead.

'These are flight simulators for training NOSA pilots,' said Captain Flare. 'Unfortunately I can't show them to you right now, as they're all being used, but I promise that you'll each get a go on one before going home on Friday afternoon.'

Everyone chattered excitedly about having the chance to use the flight simulators as Captain Flare led them out of the fitness centre and across the lawn.

'That building on the left is where you'll have your theory classes, and this is the mess,' he said, walking up some steps into a long, low building. Captain Flare held the door open for the children to step inside. The room had long, neat rows of chairs and tables, and smelled delicious.

'It doesn't look messy,' said Ralph as he walked into the mess.

Captain Flare laughed.

'Nothing on this facility is messy. Mess is the military word for dining-hall.'

'What's the military word for mess then?' asked Ralph.

'Court martial,' chuckled Captain Flare.

'What's a court martial?' Ralph whispered to Sarah once they were out of earshot of Captain Flare.

'The military word for expelled,' whispered Sarah as they sat down to lunch.

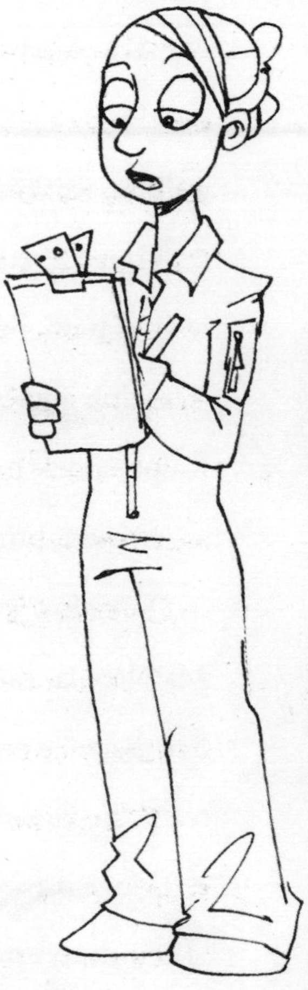

Both the main course and the dessert were so delicious that Ralph and Sarah worried that Sarah's grandmother's cake would go to waste. But they didn't have much time to dwell on it, because as soon as lunch was over, afternoon classes began.

'You have ten minutes to fetch your pencil cases and rocket designs from the dormitories and meet back at the classroom for Aerospace Engineering,' announced Ms Nebula. 'Latecomers will be punished.'

Not wanting to face latrine duty or an even worse punishment, the children ran to the dormitories and were back at the classroom with five minutes to spare.

'You're a fit little group, aren't you?' said Ms Nebula, clearly impressed. 'Now, as you know, building a rocket in a week is a pretty big task, so we'll be working in pairs.'

'Great! We can be rocket-building buddies as well as bunk buddies,' Colin said to Ralph.

Ralph and Sarah looked at each other, and Ralph shook his head. They always chose each other as partners, bunk buddies or not.

'To help you get to know one another,' continued Ms Nebula, 'rather than choose your own partner, I've assigned partners for you. This should give each team the fairest chance of winning the competition.'

'I love it when they do that!' squeaked Colin. 'They always pair the dumb kids with the smart kids. I hope I get to work with Aisling. She's the smartest girl here!'

'Shh!' hissed Aisling angrily. 'Nobody here is dumb. Everyone at Space Camp is equally smart.'

Colin looked at Ralph and rolled his eyes.

'Our first pair is Aisling Caddle and Ralph Nolan,' said Ms Nebula.

Ralph's face fell. If Colin was right, and Aisling was the smartest person at Space Camp, that meant Ms Nebula thought he was bottom of the class.

'Our next pair is Hunni Lyons and Ethelbert O'Leary,' continued Ms Nebula.

'She even thinks Bert's smarter than me,' Ralph mumbled to himself, feeling miserable.

Ms Nebula continued reading out the list of names until she came to the final pair.

'And last but not least, Sarah Monaghan and Colin Murphy. Did I miss anyone out? No? Then go and introduce yourselves to your partners and start discussing what you're going to build.'

Ralph and Sarah swapped seats.

'Remember, you only have a week to design and build your rockets, so don't try for anything too ambitious,' continued Ms Nebula. 'The rockets must be built before the real rocket launch on Friday afternoon, then we'll have our own launch. Whichever pair's rocket goes the highest, without crash-landing, will be the winner.'

Sarah and Colin immediately launched into a heated discussion about what sort of rocket to build. Neither of them thought the other had any good ideas at all, and it seemed that they would never get around to agreeing on a design, let alone building the rocket!

Around the classroom, most of the other pairs were arguing too, but at the desk next to Sarah and Colin, Aisling was busy complimenting Ralph's design.

'This is a marvellous piece of aeronautical engineering,' said Aisling. 'What material were you thinking of making it out of?'

'I hadn't really got that far,' admitted Ralph, amazed that someone as smart as Aisling liked his design.

'It'll have to be something fairly light,' said Aisling.

'Fairyfloss!' said Ralph, naming the lightest thing he could think of.

'I think fairyfloss might blow away when we launch the rocket. It'll be going pretty fast.'

'Paddlepop sticks?' suggested Ralph. 'Polystyrene?'

'It has to be something that's non-flammable,' said Aisling, 'otherwise it'll burn up on re-entry.'

Ralph looked around for inspiration and saw a fire blanket in a locker by the door.

'How about we cover it in one of those fireproof blankets, you know the ones made out of aluminium foil?' said Ralph.

'Or maybe just plain old aluminium foil,' suggested Aisling.

'Yeah!' said Ralph.

'Let's do a proper sketch,' said Aisling.

Ralph opened his pencil case and pulled out Mack. He double-clicked Mack's hat to make sure there was enough lead, and started carefully making a scale drawing of the rocket, under Aisling's instruction.

'How come Ralph's working with that new girl instead of Sarah?' Smudge asked Penny as they watched Mack fly across the paper, leaving a detailed rocket design behind him.

'I don't know,' said Penny. 'Maybe they had a fight?'

'But they're still sitting next to each other, just not working together,' observed Gloop.

'Poor Polly,' said Penny, watching Sarah scribble all over her rocket drawing and scrunch up the paper. The poor pencil in her hand looked exhausted.

A few tables away, Bert was using Cheetah to draw exactly what Hunni told him. Although Bert seemed happy enough, Cheetah was looking most annoyed at being told what to do. As Cheetah moved past Bert's pocket, Penny gasped.

'What is it, Penny?' asked Gloop.

'Look at Bert's name badge,' said Penny.

The Ethel part of Bert's name had been scribbled out in thick, black, texta ink.

'So he is here,' said Smudge.

'Nothing that we weren't expecting,' said Gloop, stiffening slightly.

'Sure,' said Penny. 'Now we just have to be prepared for anything.'

Chapter 12

Gloop to the Rescue

Penny spent the whole night and the following day in a panic. When Ralph was out of class and his pencil case in the locker, Penny would peer through the grill to make sure Black Texta wasn't making his escape. When Ralph was in class, Penny had her eyes glued to Bert's pencil case for any sign of her arch enemy. Because she was concentrating so hard on Black Texta, she missed learning about all sorts of interesting things like what would happen if you tried to land on Venus, and why some of the planets spin backwards.

But Penny's panic throughout the day was

quite unfounded. Black Texta didn't make a single appearance, and even Cheetah was behaving himself. Nevertheless, by dinner-time Penny was thoroughly exhausted.

'I don't think I have enough energy to keep watch tonight,' said Penny, lying down to rest in the back corner of the pencil case.

'You'd better get your strength back quickly,' said Gloop. 'Ralph has an evening class after dinner.'

'But that's just looking through telescopes,' yawned Penny. 'He didn't need me for Mrs Sword's evening class, so he won't need me for this one.'

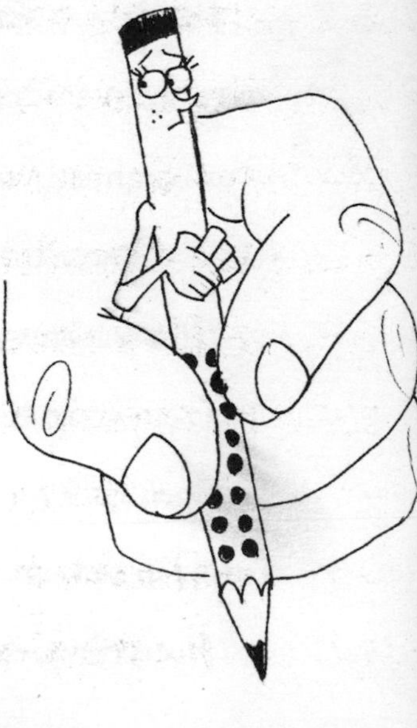

'Weren't you paying attention?' said Mack. 'The children have to write a proper scientific report at the end of it.'

'And don't forget, it was

during the last telescope class that Black Texta struck,' added Smudge.

'You guys really know how to cheer a pencil up,' said Penny sarcastically. 'I'll just have a quick rest now …'

Penny closed her eyes, and before she knew it, the pencil case was open and a red torch was shining into it.

'There you are,' said Ralph as his fingers curled around Penny and pulled her out of the pencil case.

Penny was amazed by what she saw. She was outside, in a pitch-black field, but every now and again a ghostly red telescope would appear as a child shone a torch on it to adjust the settings.

'The reason we use red torches,' the teacher, Lieutenant Stellation, was explaining, 'is so that we don't ruin our night vision. Our eyes see shapes better in red light than any other colour.

'Now, if you look above the rocket hangar you'll

see a bright star. That's Polaris, the pole star. Point your telescopes towards it.'

Ralph put Penny down on the cold ground while he fiddled with his telescope. Penny shivered.

'Now we're going to navigate, using constellations, to find a galaxy,' said Lieutenant Stellation.

'This is the best observing night ever!' said Sarah, focusing her telescope on the pole star.

'Down a bit to the west you can see a "W" for west. That's the constellation Cassiopeia,' said Lieutenant Stellation. 'If you draw an imaginary line from Polaris to the bottom star in Cassiopeia, and keep going about the same distance, you can see a fuzzy white blob. Try looking at that through your telescopes.'

With a lot of fussing and muttering under his breath, Ralph finally got the fuzzy object in focus.

'Oh my!' said Ralph.

'Isn't it beautiful?' said Aisling, who'd been gazing through her telescope at the object for a full five minutes before anyone else had managed to get it into focus.

'It's a galaxy!' said Sarah.

'That's right, it's the Andromeda galaxy,' said Lieutenant Stellation. 'It's the furthest object you can see with the naked eye.'

'How far away is it?' asked Colin.

'Two and a half million light years,' said Lieutenant Stellation.

'You mean, even travelling at the speed of light, it'd take two and a half million years to get there?' said Ralph, who'd been paying attention in Mrs Sword's planetary maths class the week before.

'Der!' said Hunni, making Bert snigger. The two of them had become good friends since being partnered together in rocket-building class, which was hardly surprising since they had a very big mean streak in common.

'Remember to write your reports up as you go,' said Lieutenant Stellation. 'And draw all the objects you observe on your star chart.'

As Mack was a far better drawer than Penny, Ralph used Mack to draw the star chart. But this time, instead of putting Penny down on the cold ground, Ralph rested her against the telescope, which gave her an excellent opportunity to look through the telescope while Ralph was busy drawing.

'It's all so beautiful,' breathed Penny. 'I wish I could go into space to see it all up close.'

As Penny looked away from the telescope, she

saw what looked like a dark shadow moving across the grass towards Ralph's star chart. She strained her eyes to look more closely, but it was too dark to see properly.

'All right, children,' said Lieutenant Stellation at the end of the lesson. 'You have an early start with Captain Flare in the morning, so please pack up.'

Ralph popped Mack and Penny back in his pencil case, then concentrated on putting his telescope back in its box, with his back turned to his workbook. Penny peered out of the pencil case, and thought she saw the same dark shadow moving away from the workbook towards Bert's pencil case. Penny poked her head out a little further to get a better view, but before she could get a proper

look, Ralph's finger pushed her gently back into the pencil case and closed the zip.

As Ralph took his pencil case and workbook back to the dormitory, Penny reported her observations to Gloop, Mack, Smudge and the space pens.

'It certainly sounds like Black Texta,' said Gloop. 'But how can we be sure?'

'The first thing,' said Penny, 'is to check Ralph's report. Black Texta tried to ruin his rocket design by scribbling on it, and I wouldn't be surprised if he tried the same thing again.'

'But how will we check it?' asked Smudge.

'Easy,' said Penny. 'As soon as the children have gone to sleep, we'll sneak out of the pencil case and have a look.'

'Aren't you forgetting something?' said Mack. 'If the children are asleep it'll be dark. How are we going to see?'

'We'll use the torch,' said Penny.

*

Ten minutes after lights out, all the children were fast asleep and Ralph's writing implements made their move. Sputink and Yuri bleeped quietly out of the pencil case in search of the torch. It was on the shelf above the pencil case and Ralph's workbook, but between the two of them they managed to lower it down to the bottom shelf without dropping it.

Penny and Mack leafed through the workbook.

'Phew!' said Penny, seeing her beautifully written

pages describing the experimental method and results untouched. 'Maybe I was seeing things.'

'No you weren't,' said Mack quietly beside her. 'Black Texta's totally ruined Ralph's star chart!'

The entire page that Ralph and Mack had drawn together was covered in so much black texta ink, it looked like a page of black paper.

'What are we going to do?' cried Penny. 'It's totally ruined.'

'Not necessarily,' said Gloop. 'Mack, can you remember what you drew tonight?'

'Every last spec of a star,' said Mack.

'Fantastic!' said Gloop. 'Talk me through it.'

*

The next morning when the children got up for their flight training class, Lieutenant Stellation was waiting at the dormitory door.

'I completely forgot last night to collect your observing reports,' he said. 'If you hand them in now, I'll have them all corrected by class time.'

Ralph and the other boys fetched their workbooks and gave them to Lieutenant Stellation.

'Enjoy flight training!' said Lieutenant Stellation, as the children headed for their morning rendezvous point outside the gym building.

'Good morning!' said Captain Flare. 'As you know, astronauts have to be extremely fit, so this morning we're having a little fitness test. We'll go for a run around the grounds, stopping at special exercise stations along the way. Follow me!'

Captain Flare set off at a cracking pace. The sleepy children found it hard to keep up with him.

After a few minutes he stopped. Some of the children doubled over, panting, as they caught up.

'No rest for the wicked,' said Captain Flare. 'Star jumps!'

Captain Flare started bouncing on the spot, throwing his legs and arms in and out.

'We'll start off easy and just do one hundred.'

'One hundred?' puffed Ralph. 'Mrs Payne was a fairy godmother compared to this guy!'

An hour later, and thoroughly exhausted, the children filed into their Astral Navigation Theory lesson.

Lieutenant Stellation was standing at the front of the classroom, beaming.

'You all performed exceptionally well in last night's exercise,' he said. 'And top marks go to …'

Everyone drew in their breath, and some even crossed their fingers.

'Ralph.'

Ralph had to pinch himself to make sure he wasn't dreaming.

'Well done, Ralph,' said Sarah.

'Way to go, bunk buddy,' said Colin.

Lieutenant Stellation walked around the classroom, handing back the workbooks. When he got to Bert he lowered his voice and said, 'You've got a bit of catching up to do. Have a look at Ralph's report to see the standard we expect at Space Camp.'

'Can I see your report please, Ralph?' said Bert with forced politeness.

'Sure!' said Ralph, opening his book to the report page, eager to see the teacher's comments.

All the children around Ralph gasped. Unlike their start charts, which were dots of grey pencil on a white background, Ralph's page looked like the real night sky, with white stars on a black background. None of the children were more surprised than Ralph.

'How clever, to draw the stars with correction fluid!' said Aisling. 'How'd you come up with that?'

'I have absolutely no idea,' said a stunned Ralph.

'Well, there's no doubt about it. I'm partnered with the most enlightened learner at Space Camp!' said Aisling, giving Ralph a kiss on the cheek.

Ralph looked away in embarrassment, and noticed Sarah glaring at him through narrowed eyes.

'Don't blame me,' said Ralph. 'What do you care anyway? You're going to marry Rick O'Shea.'

Chapter 13

Transit of Mercury

Sarah's mood did not improve throughout Astral Navigation, and got even worse when Ms Nebula appeared to tell them that Aerospace Engineering had been swapped with Planetary Science due to a 'significant astronomical event' taking place that afternoon. Ralph spent the whole of Aerospace Engineering trying not to talk to Aisling – which was very difficult since they were rocket-building partners – as every time he and Aisling said anything to each other, Sarah would growl.

Eventually Colin managed to snap Sarah out of it by yelling, 'If you spent half as much time looking

at our rocket as you do looking at their rocket, we might actually get somewhere!'

By lunchtime the four of them were friends again and very excited about what the significant astronomical event could be.

'An eclipse!' said Colin.

'I don't think so,' said Aisling, looking out the window purposefully. 'Eclipses only happen during the day when the moon passes in front of the sun, and I can't see the moon.'

'It's Planetary Science,' said Sarah, 'so it's got to be something to do with a planet.'

'Maybe a spacecraft's landing on Mars,' suggested Ralph.

'Nah,' said Colin. 'I get *Mission Monthly*, which is a magazine that talks about all the latest planetary spacecraft and when they're supposed to land on planets, or do a fly-by. There's nothing scheduled for this month at all, on any of the planets.'

'What else could it be?' said Sarah.

They spent the rest of lunch-time discussing it, and were quite excited by the time Ursula Major appeared in the mess hall to tell them the lesson

was being held in the observation field instead of the classroom.

'Has anybody guessed what the significant astronomical event could be?' asked Ursula Major.

Hunni put up her hand.

'Bert and I were discussing it at lunch-time, and we concluded that it must be a transit of one of the inferior planets.'

Ralph, Sarah, Aisling and Colin all looked at each other.

'That's absolutely right,' said Ursula Major. 'You'll all remember from our first lesson that planets that are closer to the sun than the Earth are called inferior planets, and that a transit is when the planet passes in front of the sun. Can anybody guess which planet is transiting this afternoon?'

'Venus!' said Colin.

'I'm sorry, Colin. It's the other one,' said Ursula Major.

'Mer-cur-eeeeee,' said Bert in a sing-song voice.

'No prizes for guessing that one,' muttered Aisling.

'We'll be using telescopes to watch the transit this afternoon, and I don't need to tell you to never, ever look at the sun through a telescope or binoculars,' continued Ursula Major. 'Did anybody not do sunspot observations during Space Week at school?'

None of the children spoke.

'Good,' said Ursula Major. 'Then you all know how to set up your telescopes, with your workbooks behind the eyepiece to catch the image of the sun. Make sure you focus your telescopes properly – we don't want you burning a hole in your workbook! We have lots of flammable chemicals on the base, so any risk of fire, however small, is very serious. And remember, this is an experimental report, so you must write everything down as you go along.'

Ralph opened his pencil case and pulled out Penny. She was instantly on the look-out for Black Texta, and searched through the children's faces until she found Bert. But almost as worrying as the threat of Black Texta was the I'm-up-to-something look on Bert's face.

Penny squinted closely at Bert, who was holding his workbook very close to the eyepiece of his telescope and focusing the light into a very small spot. Moments later the paper started smoking, and burst into flame.

'Ethelbert O'Leary!' thundered Ursula Major's voice from the front of the class. 'Put your telescope away at once! You are banned from this exercise. Go and report to Captain Flare for latrine duty ... in the girls' toilets!'

Penny watched warily as Bert gathered his things and stalked off towards Captain Flare's quarters, and was pleased to see that he hadn't left anything big and black behind.

'It's started!' said Colin from the telescope next to Ralph's. 'Mercury's crossing the sun!'

'What?' said Ursula Major, looking at her watch. 'It's not due to start for another twenty-three minutes.'

'I can see sunspots, but there's nothing transiting,' said Sarah, adjusting her focus.

'Same here,' said Aisling.

'Now instead of going sideways, it's going up the sun!' said Colin, marking everything down in his workbook like a good scientist. 'And now it's doing a little circle!'

By this time Ursula Major had reached Colin's telescope and started laughing.

'I don't mean to laugh, but look at your telescope,' she said to Colin.

Colin bent to peer through the eye-piece, but faster than lightning, Ursula Major had yanked his head away from it.

'I said at it, not through it,' she said, pointing to the wide end of the telescope.

A little ladybird had landed on the lens and was going for a bit of an explore. Colin had mistaken the ladybird for Mercury.

'Oops!' said Colin.

'Never mind,' said Ursula Major. 'Come on everybody. We've only got twenty-one minutes until it starts.'

By the time the transit was due to start, all the

other NOSA instructors and many of the staff had come out onto the lawn to watch.

'How come they're so interested in our experiment?' said Ralph.

'Transits of Mercury are quite rare,' said Aisling. 'They only happen roughly once every ten years.'

'I guess that's why they call it a significant astronomical event,' said Sarah.

'Even Captain Flare's let Bert off latrine duty so he can watch it,' observed Colin, pointing to where Bert and Captain Flare were standing by Hunni's telescope.

During Mercury's crossing of the sun, Penny was kept busy tracing the planet's path and writing down the exact time when the planet reached certain points.

When the transit was over, the really hard work began. After the children had packed up their telescopes, Ursula Major took them back to the classroom where they had to work out how large the sun was and how far away it was from the Earth by using some very complicated maths. Even Bert had to do the hard part, sharing Hunni's measurements.

At the end of the lesson Ursula Major collected the children's workbooks and whisked them away for correction before Black Texta could do any damage to them.

'Now unless Ursula Major corrects them sitting in the girls' latrines, I think we're safe on this one,' said Gloop.

But despite Gloop's assurance, Penny felt uneasy. It wasn't like Black Texta to give up on one of his evil plans so easily, and Penny couldn't shake the feeling that he had something even more dastardly up his casing.

Chapter 14

Sabotage

By morning break on Friday the children's minds were reeling. Gemma Nigh's Advanced Relativity class had been far too advanced for this particular group of enlightened learners.

'I didn't understand and word of that,' said Ralph.

'Was she even speaking English?' asked Colin.

'I think even Einstein himself would have had trouble understanding that – and he invented relativity!' said Aisling.

'I'm just glad it's over,' said Sarah. 'We've only got one more rocket-building class and it's our last chance! Colin, I was thinking …'

Sarah and Colin spent the whole of lunch-time discussing improvements to their rocket, and for once in his life Ralph was pleased not to be working with Sarah. Aisling was far more relaxed about things and spent lunch-time talking about television shows like *Officer Cool* – which was also her favourite – and how to get passed level eight on her favourite computer game *Ecowarrior*.

Aerospace Engineering that afternoon was frantic. Everyone was hurrying to put the finishing touches on their rockets, and Ms Nebula had to run from one pair to another to answer their final questions. Even Aisling snapped at Ralph on occasion, but she always apologised afterwards.

Towards the end of the lesson, Ms Nebula was constantly glancing at her watch, and with some relief finally clapped her hands together and said, 'That's it, children. It's time to stop working and go and watch the rocket launch.'

The children put down their pencils and rocket-building tools and left the classroom. Once the coast was clear, Penny and the others jumped up and ran to the windowsill so that they could watch the rocket launch too. Even though the launch pad was very far away, the rocket was so big that the pencils could see it easily.

'I'm so excited!' said Penny. 'We've been learning all about space for the last two weeks, and now we get to see the launch of a real space craft!'

'What about the rockets Ralph and Sarah have been working on all week?' said Polly, who had popped out of Sarah's pencil case to join them on the windowsill.

'But they're not really going into space,' said Penny. 'I mean, the kids are smart, but they're hardly rocket scientists.'

'Shh!' said Smudge. 'They're starting the countdown.'

As the afternoon sun streamed in through the window, the flight director's voice boomed over the loud speaker.

'Ten … nine …'

Steam started to pour out of the engines at the base of the rocket.

'Eight … seven …'

Little jets of flame shot out of the bottom.

'Six … five …'

The ground started to shake.

'Four … three …'

The engines roared into life and even from all the way back in the classroom the pencils had to put their hands over their ears.

'Two … one …'

The rocket started to shudder.

'Blast-off!'

The rocket moved upwards, slowly at first but getting faster and faster the higher it went, steam

and flames pouring out of its engines.

'Wow!' said Penny. 'You can even smell the smoke and feel the heat of the flames from back here!'

Polly sniffed the air, then turned away from the window and screamed.

'Ralph's rocket's on fire!' she yelled.

All the pencils whirled around. Black Texta was standing on the edge of Ralph's desk, holding a telescope lens up to the beam of afternoon sunlight. He was using the lens to focus the light into a small point on Ralph's rocket, and just like Bert's workbook, it was in flames.

'No!' cried Penny, as Black Texta looked up at her and laughed.

'Get him!' said Mack, leaping off the windowsill.

Black Texta moved the lens so that it shone sunlight into the pencils' eyes.

'I can't see a thing!' yelled Polly.

'Where did he go?' bellowed Mack, who had missed the desk and landed painfully on the floor.

'Forget him,' cried Penny. 'We have to save Ralph's rocket!'

The pencils ran into each other blindly in their

efforts to get to the flames. Above the roar of the fire they suddenly heard a bleep … bleep … bleeping coming from the front of the classroom. Sputink and Yuri were flying towards Ralph's

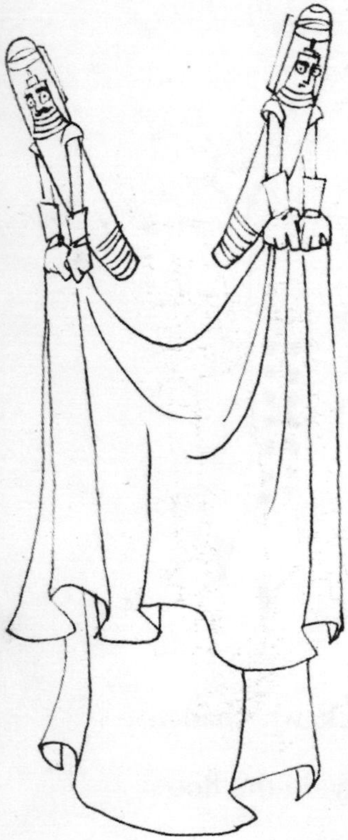

rocket, carrying the fire blanket with them. When they were directly over the rocket, they dropped the blanket and the flames went out instantly.

Penny ran towards the rocket to inspect the damage.

'Wait!' cried Gloop. 'It'll be too hot to touch. Give it a moment to cool.'

The pencils gathered around the remains of the rocket and waited for Gloop's okay. When it was safe enough to touch, Sputink and Yuri raised the fire blanket. All that was underneath were the charred remains of Ralph and Aisling's rocket.

'How could you do such a thing?' Penny yelled at Black Texta, who was hovering a safe distance away on Bert's desk.

'Don't look at me,' said Black Texta. 'This is all your fault.'

'My fault? How?' asked Penny.

'If you hadn't interfered with my first little plan, then Ralph would never have come to Space Camp, and would never have built that rocket,' said Black Texta. 'Try explaining that to his partner's pencils.'

All Aisling's pencils were poking their heads out of Aisling's pencil case, looking very sad indeed.

'All her fault,' Black Texta shouted to Aisling's pencils, pointing at Penny.

'How dare you blame me for something you did out of spite!' Penny yelled.

'I'll do whatever I like,' boomed Black Texta, drawing himself up to his full height and flexing his

enormous muscles. Even from a few desks away, he was a terrifying sight.

'You're in quite a fix now, aren't you, Penny Pencil? You can't write or draw your way out of this one, and it's going to take a bit more than a few drops of correction fluid to repair it,' continued Black Texta, narrowing his eyes at Gloop. 'Good luck trying!' he added, disappearing into Bert's pencil case where the sound of party music could clearly be heard.

'Well, that's that then,' said Polly. 'He really has beaten us this time.'

Penny looked around the classroom sadly. All the other children's finished rockets lay on the desks, gleaming in the afternoon sunlight, surrounded by tools and left-over pieces of rocket materials.

'No he hasn't!' said Penny. 'We still have the design, and if we all work together, using the left-overs from the other children's rockets, we can rebuild it!'

The others looked at her doubtfully.

'And we'll help,' said a voice from among the left-overs.

A pile of papers rose up and shook itself, to reveal a friendly-looking family of spanners underneath.

'We'll all help,' said a screwdriver, gesturing to himself, a saw and a hammer.

'Only problem is, it might be a bit noisy,' said the drill.

'That's okay,' said Penny. 'It doesn't matter how much noise we make. The party music in Bert's pencil case will drown it out. Black Texta won't hear a thing!'

'You're right,' said the leader of Aisling's pencils. 'We're in.'

'Us too,' said Gloop.

'I'll round up some of Sarah's pencils as well,' said Polly. 'We'll show that Black Texta that we're a force to be reckoned with!'

Chapter 15

Blast-off!

Just like the real NOSA rocket hangar, the classroom was soon filled with the sounds of sawing, hammering and drilling as Penny and her friends rebuilt Ralph and Aisling's rocket.

'And now for the finishing touch,' said Penny, holding up a piece of special rocket glass, 'the window!'

Penny placed the rocket glass in front of the window frame, but her face fell.

'Oh, no! It's too small. Do we have a bigger piece?'

'Unless we pull the window out of Bert's rocket, which I'd love to do,' said Mack, 'no.'

‘This is terrible!’ said Penny. ‘It won’t seal properly, and it’ll burn up on re-entry.’

‘We could stick more adhesive over it …’ suggested Smudge.

‘That won’t work either,’ said the spanner, who had the most experience in rocket-building. ‘The outer surface needs to be smooth.’

‘Actually, the adhesive will work,’ said Penny, ‘if we stick it on the inside.’

'But then someone would have to be inside the rocket ...' began Polly.

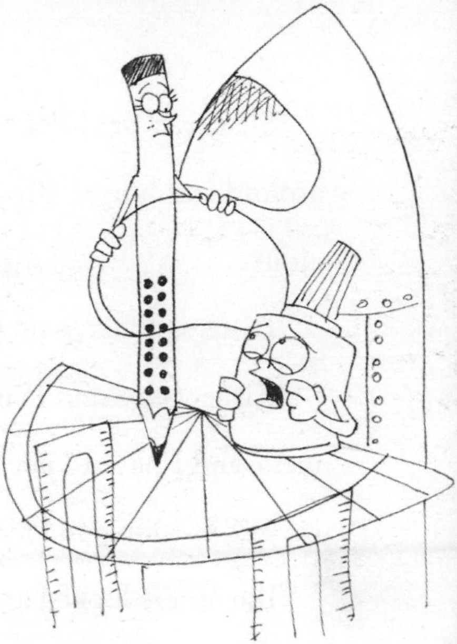

'And whoever it was, wouldn't be able to get out,' said Gloop.

'I know,' said Penny quietly.

All of Ralph, Sarah and Aisling's pencils stared at her.

'You mean ...?' said Mack.

'Yep. I'm volunteering,' said Penny.

'But you can't,' said Gloop. 'It's too dangerous. The rocket could explode on take-off, burn up on re-entry, crash land ...'

'There might be some danger involved,' conceded Penny.

'Some danger?' said Mack. 'It's bordering on suicidal!'

'So what?' said Penny. 'Maybe if I wasn't around any longer Black Texta would leave Ralph alone.'

'Don't say that,' said Gloop.

'Either way,' said Penny. 'I got Ralph into this mess, and I have to get him out of it. We've all worked too long and too hard to give up now.'

The others looked at each other uneasily.

'If you're sure,' said Polly.

Penny nodded.

Sputink bleeped his way over to Penny.

'Here,' he said, taking off his helmet and passing it to Penny, 'this'll keep you safe.'

'Thanks, Sputink,' said Penny, popping the helmet on her head.

'And take this,' said Yuri, slipping his communicator off his wrist and putting it on Penny's. 'This way we'll be able to keep in touch.'

'Thanks, Yuri,' said Penny.

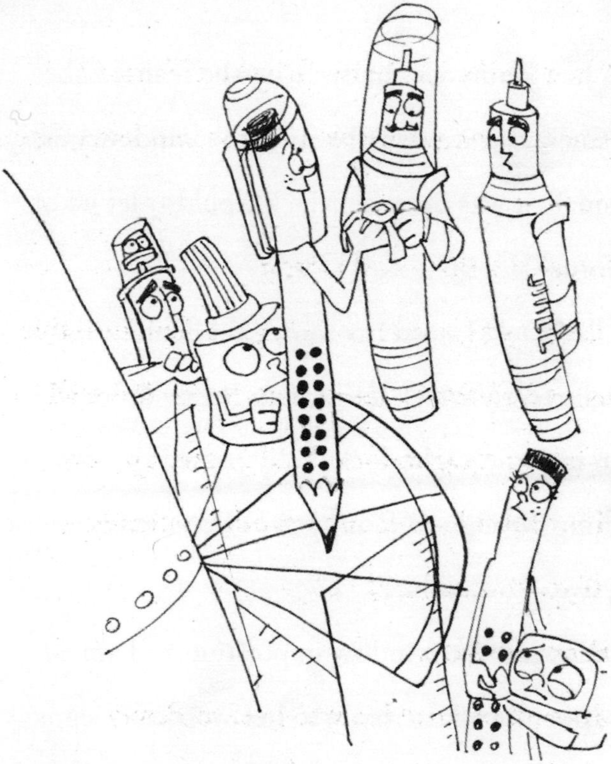

'And you take mine,' said Sputink, passing his communicator to Gloop.

'Need a boost?' asked Mack, as Penny made her way towards the rocket.

'Thanks,' said Penny, stepping on Mack's hands as he lifted her high enough to climb through the window frame.

When Penny was halfway in, she realised she was stuck. But it wasn't because the window was too small, it was because Mack wouldn't let go of her foot.

'Uh, Mack. I need my foot,' said Penny.

Reluctantly Mack let go, and Penny dropped down into the flight deck. Polly passed the window carefully through to Penny, and Gloop gave her the adhesive.

Penny put the window in position and sealed it up. She waved excitedly to her worried friends outside the rocket.

All of a sudden the pencils scattered, which could only mean one thing – the children were arriving.

Penny pressed herself up against the wall next to the window, so that if Ralph or Aisling looked inside their rocket they wouldn't be able to see her.

'Okay, children. Gather your rockets and take them to the launch site,' said Ms Nebula.

Very carefully, Ralph and Aisling picked up their rocket between them. They thought they were keeping it very steady as they carried it outside to the launch site, but inside the rocket Penny was rolling around like a pencil in an empty pencil case.

'I hope I don't get space-sick,' Penny thought as she rattled from one side of the flight deck to the other, doing her best to keep away from the window.

Once the children had left the classroom, all their pencils and the rocket-building tools leaped up and ran over to the windowsill. Each of them wanted to see how well the rocket that they'd helped design and build performed.

Even Bert's pencils and textas climbed onto the windowsill to look.

When Ralph and Aisling reached the launch site, they carefully set the rocket up, ready for blast-off. Penny took the last of the adhesive tape and fastened herself to the wall for the take-off.

'All right,' said Ms Nebula, 'we'll start with Colin and Sarah's rocket. Commence ignition sequence!'

Colin and Sarah counted backwards from ten. On zero, their rocket shot up into the air. All the children, as well as Colin and Sarah's pencils, held their breath as the rocket cruised through the air.

'He-herm,' said a rude voice behind Mack, Gloop and Smudge.

They turned around. It was Black Texta.

'Good of you to turn up to cheer on the other rockets,' said Black Texta sarcastically. 'I trust you'll be shouting for Bert and Hunni.'

'Hardly,' said Gloop, turning back to watch the progress of Colin and Sarah's rocket, which was very high in the sky, and keeping his communicator hidden from Black Texta.

'I see that Penny didn't make it. Too busy sulking?' enquired Black Texta.

'You'll be the one sulking, Black Texta,' said Mack.

There was a round of applause from the rocket-testing site, as Colin and Sarah's rocket parachuted down to a perfect landing.

'Next,' announced Ms Nebula, 'we have Ralph and Aisling.'

'What?' said Black Texta, throwing himself against the window-pane so he could see better. Sure enough, Ralph and Aisling had a shiny, exact copy of the rocket Black Texta had burned to a crisp less than an hour ago.

'How …?' said Black Texta.

He turned around and looked at all Ralph, Sarah and Aisling's pencils who were smiling at him innocently (and only trembling a little).

'Penny Pencil,' said Black Texta under his breath. 'Where is she?' he demanded, grabbing Polly by the throat.

Polly shook her head.

'I won't ask you again, WHERE IS SHE?' demanded Black Texta, tightening his grip.

'The rocket ...' gasped Polly.

Black Texta dropped Polly and bounded out of the classroom.

'Stop him!' cried Mack, running after him.

'No!' yelled Gloop. 'We can't! We're not allowed

to move around if we can be seen. We might bump into stray humans out there.'

'But Penny …' cried Mack, as Sputink and Yuri gently pulled him away from the classroom door.

'Penny … Penny! Come in!' said Gloop, speaking into his communicator.

'What is it, Gloop?' Penny's voice crackled back. 'I'm all strapped in and they're about to start the countdown.'

Outside at the launch site, Ralph and Aisling were counting down.

'Ten!' said Ralph.

'Nine!' said Aisling.

'Black Texta's on his way!' said Gloop.

'Eight!'

'What?' said Penny, looking out the rocket window nervously. A huge, black object was moving quickly across the lawn towards her.

'Seven!'

'Black Texta's on his way,' repeated Gloop.

'Six!'

'I know, I can see him,' said Penny, swallowing hard and willing the countdown to speed up.

'Five!'

The rocket motor turned on, almost drowning out the sound of the countdown.

'Four!'

'Can't you do anything to stop him?' said Penny desperately, as Black Texta drew closer.

'Three!'

'There are too many people about,' said Gloop. 'You know the rules.'

'Two!'

'Rules,' said Penny, gritting her teeth as the rocket started vibrating, 'are over-rated.'

'One!'

'Penny Penciiiiiiiiiiiiiiil!' howled Black Texta, hurling himself at the rocket.

'Blastoff!'

The rocket shuddered and shook and shot upwards. Penny peered out the window, through the flames and swirling toxic gas clouds, and saw Black Texta writhing on the grass, his casing all bubbled and split.

'Penny! What's happening?' Gloop's voice squeaked through the communicator.

'Everything's fine,' said Penny through chattering teeth.

'What about Black Texta?'

'It appears he's too exhausted to follow me into space,' said Penny, turning her attention from the black puddle on the grass below, to the view above.

The sky was turning from pale blue, to dark blue and then to black. Penny rubbed her eyes to make sure she wasn't seeing things and looked out the window again. Yes! She could really see stars! She was in space!

'This is amazing!' she said into her communicator. 'I can see stars!'

All the pencils and tools back at Mission Control in the classroom cheered.

'Sputink's just told me that if you can see stars,' said Gloop, 'it's safe to take off your seatbelt.'

Carefully, Penny peeled off the adhesive tape that was securing her to the wall and watched it float

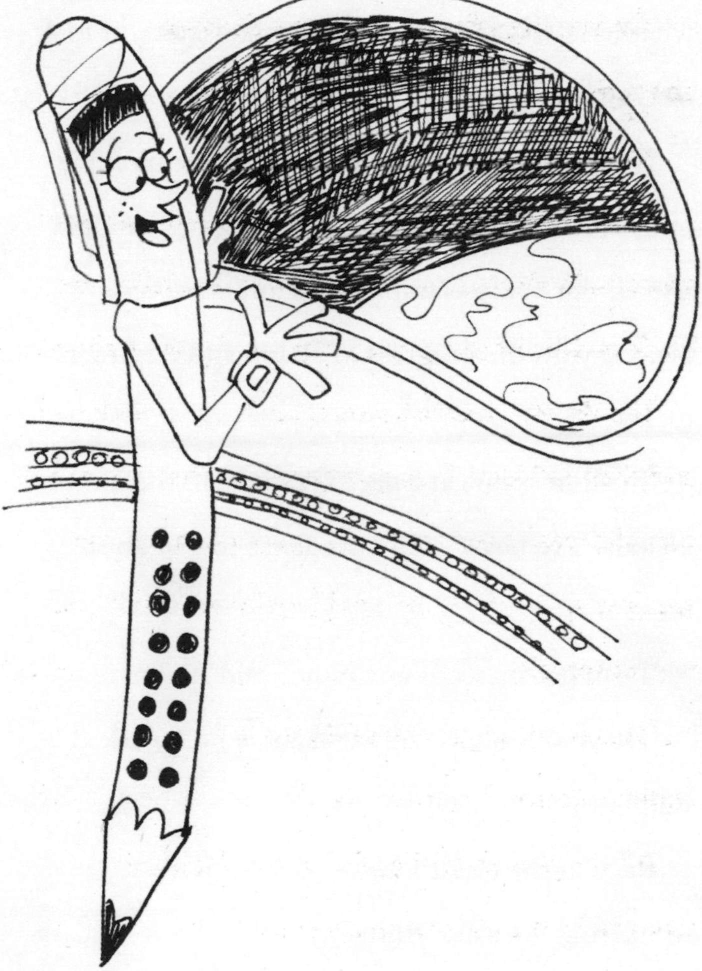

away from her. She took a step and floated around the flight deck. She really was weightless.

'This is the best feeling ever!' said Penny, unsure

whether it was more fun to do somersaults, or look out the window at the pretty space scene.

Not only were the pencils and rocket-building tools at Mission Control excited, but the children and all the Space Camp instructors were very pleased with the progress of Ralph and Aisling's rocket.

'In all my years at Space Camp,' said Stella Nebula, 'I've never seen a student's rocket go so high.'

'I can hardly see it any more,' said Aisling.

'Do you think it really will come back?' asked Ralph.

Back in the classroom the pencils were wondering the same thing.

Chapter 16

Re-entry

'Penny – are you okay?' asked Gloop.

'Never better,' said Penny, thoroughly enjoying herself. 'The stars are even prettier up here. There are so many of them! And – oh!'

Penny broke off suddenly as a large, metallic object with several antennae whizzed by the window.

'What's wrong?' yelled Gloop.

'I just flew by a satellite, and it startled me,' said Penny, to the relief of all her friends back at Mission Control.

Penny looked back down at the Earth, where

she could clearly see the whole country of Ireland surrounded by ocean.

'The view from up here is amazing,' she said. 'Can you still see me?'

'No,' said Gloop. 'Are you still going up?'

'It's hard to tell,' said Penny, peering out the window. Then she realised that her face was pressed up hard against the glass, and it took all her energy to pull herself away. Suddenly she felt very heavy.

'Uh-oh. Something feels different,' she said into her communicator.

But all they heard back at Mission Control was 'uh-oh', followed by a hiss of static.

'Penny? Penny! What's going on?' Gloop yelled into the communicator, but he only got static in reply.

Polly, Mack and Smudge looked at each other anxiously.

'Could the communicator be out of range?' Gloop asked Sputink and Yuri.

'No,' said Sputink. 'But there's often a communication black-out during re-entry.'

'So she's on her way back?' asked Mack.

'I'd say so,' said Sputink.

'Girls, we'd better get busy,' said Polly, leading all the coloured pencils back to the desk.

'What are you doing with that?' asked Mack, as they busied themselves decorating a huge silver sign.

'Isn't it obvious?' said Polly. 'Making a "Welcome Back" banner.'

'No!' said Mack more urgently. 'What are you doing with *that*?'

All the pencils and tools on the windowsill turned around. Mack was very pale, pointing at the large piece of aluminium foil the coloured pencils were decorating.

'That's the heat-proof shield that's supposed to be on Penny's rocket, to stop it burning up on re-entry,' said Mack weakly.

The pencils and tools looked from the heat shield to each other in horror. The only sound that

could be heard was the static hissing from the communicator on Gloop's wrist.

'Penny! Penny! If you can hear me, come in!' yelled Gloop into the communicator.

Up in the rocket, Penny couldn't hear anything but the roaring of the rocket as it ploughed back into the Earth's atmosphere. The rocket plummeted faster and faster until it suddenly stopped.

'Penny!' squawked Gloop's voice from the communicator. 'Please come in!'

Exhausted, Penny raised her wrist to her mouth and said, 'I'm here.'

All the pencils and rocket-building tools at Mission Control held their breath.

'What can you see?' asked Gloop.

Penny peered out the window.

She could see the grounds of NOSA directly below her, including the landing pad with a big X in the middle of it.

'I'm just above NOSA,' she said.

'Look! There she is!' said Smudge, pointing out the window at the rocket, which was hanging in the air under a red and white striped parachute.

All the pencils and rocket-building tools cheered, as did the children and Space Camp instructors out on the lawn.

They all watched the craft glide gently to touch down in the middle of the landing pad.

'Well done, Penny,' said Gloop.

'Well done, Ralph and Aisling,' said Stella Nebula.

The other children launched their rockets one by one, but none of them flew as high as the one the pencils had built, and at the end of the afternoon Ms Nebula awarded Ralph and Aisling a rocket-shaped trophy.

'Do you want to keep the trophy?' Aisling asked Ralph.

'No, you should keep it,' said Ralph.

'Then you get to keep the rocket,' insisted Aisling.

*

When Ralph arrived home from Space Camp that evening, he cleared a space on the top of his bookshelf for the rocket to stand in pride of place.

'Ralph! Dinner's ready!' his mother called.

Ralph took one final look at the rocket, puffed his chest out proudly and ran downstairs.

The second he was gone, Gloop, Mack, Smudge and the space pens leaped out of Ralph's pencil case and climbed to the top of the bookshelf. They tapped gently on the window of the rocket.

'It's okay to come out now, Penny,' said Gloop.

Penny undid the adhesive tape along the bottom

and sides of the window so that the glass swung open like a cat flap. She climbed out, letting the window flap shut behind her, the adhesive tape sealing it closed with a soft *fttt*!

'Well done, Penny!' said Mack.

'That was a brilliant plan of yours,' said Gloop approvingly, 'with only one flaw,' he continued, looking at her sternly.

'What's that?' asked Penny innocently.

Gloop pushed against the window, but the adhesive tape held it shut fast.

'The window's sealed just as tightly now as it was when you were inside the rocket,' said Gloop, making Penny's cheeks flush. 'There was no real need for you to go up into space at all, was there?'

'Yes there was!' said Smudge.

Penny and Gloop stared at him.

'If Penny hadn't been in the rocket, Black Texta wouldn't have run after her, and she wouldn't have been able to get him with the exhaust, right Penny?' said Smudge, full of admiration.

'Er, right,' said Penny. 'That was my plan all long,' she lied, smiling innocently at Gloop.

'What are we going to do with you?' said Gloop, shaking his head.

'Have a party!' said Mack.

And with that the space pens picked Penny up and flew her back to the pencil case where the 'Welcome back to Earth' party – complete with shiny, silver banner – was in full swing.

Penny

Other books in the

Penny the Pencil series …

Coming June 2010

Penny the Pencil is a clever little pencil who is very good at spelling and sums, but not so good at remembering the pencil-case rules:

- **Rule Number One:** no talking while the zip is open.
- **Rule Number Two:** no correcting spelling mistakes.
- **Rule Number Three:** anyone who breaks the rules will be expelled.

When the nasty Black Texta and his sidekick Rubber catch Penny helping her owner with a spelling test, terrible events unfold …

Penny the Pencil * Eileen O'Hely * ISBN: 978 1 85635 475 2

Having overthrown Black Texta and his evil sidekick Rubber, Penny and her friends can get on with helping Ralph with his schoolwork.

But someone is writing graffiti on Ralph's school books and vandalising Sarah's entry in the school colouring competition.

With help from Sarah's pencil Polly, Penny goes undercover to find out who is committing these dastardly deeds. After close calls in the pencil cases of Lucy the Stealer and Seán the Chewer, Penny and Polly stumble across the lair of the evil culprit, and discover that it will take all their ingenuity to save not only themselves, but all the children in Ralph's class from the evil plot.

Penny Goes Undercover ⁎ **Eileen O'Hely** ⁎ **ISBN: 978 1 85635 518 6**

Penny can't believe her luck. She told everyone she was going to become a TV star and now it's really happening! *Officer Cool* is Ralph's favourite TV show and now Penny is to be his trusted side-kick, Officer Lead.

But someone has been tampering with the scripts and Penny has a feeling that the evil Black Texta is behind it all. Penny's plan to run a competition during the show just might save the day, but when Bert the Bully wins the competition, she begins to get suspicious …

With the help of her new friends Clappers the clapperboard, Ruby the make-up brush and Meg the megaphone, Penny has to give the performance of her life if she is going to stop the show from being cancelled.

Penny the Star * **Eileen O'Hely** * **ISBN: 978 1 85635 542 1**

It is Health Awareness Month in Ralph's school. The new arrival in the pencil case, Baron de Couberpen, is whipping the pencils into shape for the inaugural Pencilympics. But even before the Pencilympic flame is lit, the competition takes a terrible turn when Cheetah the Cheater almost drowns during training for the rowing race.

When things start to go wrong in the classroom Penny suspects she knows who is behind the sinister sabotage. She realises that she might have to sacrifice her dreams of Pencilympic glory if she is to defeat her old enemy ... Black Texta!

Penny the Athlete * **Eileen O'Hely** * **ISBN: 978 1 85635 570 4**